Wendy Sparrow

THE HIPPO POOL

THE HIPPO POOL

W. V. Squair

Book Guild Publishing
Sussex, England

First published in Great Britain in 2009 by
The Book Guild Ltd
Pavilion View
19 New Road
Brighton
BN1 1UF

Typesetting in Baskerville by
Nat-Type, Cheshire

Printed in Great Britain by
CPI Antony Rowe

A catalogue record for this book is available from
The British Library.

ISBN 978 1 84624 304 2

1

He pushed his dugout canoe into the river and paddled towards the pools. In the twilight the small islands that surrounded them were just visible. He stopped close to one of them; the canoe hardly drifted in this slow-moving part of the river. Picking up his torch he shone it on the water. A myriad cichlids rushed towards the surface, attracted by the light. Using his small net Mahachi scooped up the tiny fish and put them into one of his containers. Throughout the night he paddled slowly around the islands, until he had caught enough fish to feed his family with some to spare. As he felt the cold hour before dawn approach, he stopped fishing and waited until the fierce African sun burst above the horizon.

Great roly-poly bodies with short fat legs made enormous splashes as they entered the water, returning to the river after a night of grazing. Once the hippopotamuses were submerged near the long island, Mahachi paddled safely to the shore and hid his canoe in the bushes, covering it with plastic mealie meal bags and hessian sacks. Then he walked along the dirt road back to his village carrying his heavy load.

Entering the village he walked to the fire in the cooking area where Amai, his mother, was already preparing the breakfast. He put his containers on the ground beside her. She looked down. 'You have a good catch Mahachi; there is plenty for everyone. The fish will make a tasty relish.' She handed him a large bowl of mealie meal porridge made from maize. 'Here eat this, my son, you must be hungry after your night's work.'

'Yes, Amai, I am. There were so many small fish tonight. If Chikomo had been with me I could have filled more containers.'

'He is too young for night fishing, Mahachi. Chikomo is still a boy but you are almost a man.'

Amai looked at Mahachi; she had nothing but pride and admiration for him. She knew all about the perils of the great river, especially at night. Midstream it was treacherous, the swift running water led to the Victoria Falls and certain death. *Mosi-oa-Tunya* was the name their people used for The Falls, the smoke that thunders. Amai was glad that Mahachi worked in the relative safety of the pools, away from the rocky areas and sandbanks where crocodiles liked to bask.

Ambuya joined them by the fire. 'Your catch is more than enough for us to eat, Mahachi. We can dry some. The bream will be spawning soon, then we shall have fine big fish to eat.' He smiled at her. Ambuya looked at her handsome grandson. When he was a child she used to carry him on her back while she worked in the fields; the bond between them had grown strong. Now he was almost a man and a skilled fisherman. 'You look tired,' she said, concerned. 'After you have eaten you should go and rest.'

When Mahachi reached his rondavel, Chikomo was waiting for him. Chikomo wanted to be a good fisherman like his brother. 'Why can I not come with you when you fish at night, Mahachi?'

'Amai says you are too young yet ...'

'Ooh,' said Chikomo, sounding disgruntled.

'... but Ambuya thinks there will be bream to catch soon; I will be fishing during the day, then you can come with me.' Chikomo beamed with delight. 'But you must promise to do as I say.'

2

'I will Mahachi, I will.'

'Now I need to sleep, I am exhausted.'

Chikomo slipped away. He was anxious to please his brother.

The village where Mahachi lived was in the Zambezi Valley. With so much water nearby there was always plenty growing in the fields but his people kept no cattle, only goats and chicken. The valley was the home of the tsetse fly, deadly to cattle. With none to tend, some boys herded goats and others learnt to fish.

When he was a boy Mahachi had been taught to fish by his father, Baba. He remembered how eager he had been to accompany his father each time he went fishing and, like Chikomo, how disappointed he had felt when his pleas to go out with him at night had initially been rejected. It had taken Mahachi a long time to learn the skills of negotiating such a large and dangerous river.

Several days later Mahachi and Chikomo stood eating a bowl full of steaming porridge, before setting off early in search of bream.

'Mahachi, I have wrapped some bread in paper for each of you. Where will you go today?'

'We will go to the Hippo Pool, Amai, and see what we can find in the shallows nearby.'

The two boys each carried a container and a freshly sharpened spear made from the strong bamboo-like reeds that grew by the river. The road they took was thickly wooded. Along the way, green lovebirds with rosy pink faces and colourful, black-cheeked parakeets flitted from tree to tree. Their shrill chattering sounded like angry disagreements. Chikomo stopped by the old baobab, a giant among African trees. 'I am going to search for some fruit to take with us.'

'Do not be long, we have much to do.'

The enormous girth of the baobab was covered in smooth

3

grey bark. Chikomo searched the ground for its large, egg-shaped fruits with khaki suede-like skins. 'Here are some, they are still whole.' Chikomo put them in his container with the bread. 'Now we have plenty to eat.'

After a while, a clearing appeared in the trees to the left and Mahachi and his brother walked down to the banks of the mighty Zambezi. Out in the river, not far from the bank, was the long island; in between was the Hippo Pool. The hippos had already returned from their nocturnal feeding. Their rotund bodies were immersed in deep water, only their heads could be seen. Occasionally one of them would yawn, revealing huge jagged teeth set in a mouth incongruously lined with a delicate, feminine shade of pink.

Mahachi and Chikomo took their spears and walked into the shallow water along the very edge of the river, to begin their search for the coveted bream.

After a while Mahachi called out, 'Over here Chikomo, I have found some.' They both looked into the clear water and watched a pair of bream begin their fatiguing dance. 'We must be patient and wait until they have finished.'

They watched as the mating pair worked in a circle. Using their tails the fish rapidly fanned the sandy bottom to create a small indentation in the river bed. Then they began the long process of depositing the fertilised eggs there. This done, they used their tails to cover the eggs with sand, which protected them until they hatched. The bream were now exhausted. Barely able to move, they rested from their labours.

'Now we can strike,' whispered Mahachi. With a quick thrust they pinioned the weakened fish on to the point of their spears.

'This one is really big,' cried Mahachi delightedly.

'Mine is smaller but still a good size.' Chikomo was a little disappointed. They stored the bream in their containers on the bank and returned to the shallows. In the pool a hippo raised its head and grunted repeatedly.

4

'I think we should rest for a while,' said Mahachi as the sun rose in the sky to the noon position. 'Let us sit in the shade and eat our bread.' In the water the only parts of the hippos still visible looked like large grey boulders.

When they had finished eating their bread Chikomo broke open one of the baobab fruits. The segments containing a white pulp were slightly acidic, refreshing their mouths as they sucked them. The flavour was very pleasing. They relaxed, savouring the sherbet-like taste. Opposite them on the long island, a herd of elephants silently meandered through the long grass towards the tall palms which bore vegetable ivory. The hard brown fruits, containing an ivory-nut, were a favourite with the elephants and they searched on the ground for fallen ones.

'Come on Chikomo, it is time we started looking for more fish. How many do we have so far?'

Chikomo looked into the containers. 'I have two and you have three, five altogether.'

'Let us see how many we can find before the sun begins to set.'

They stepped into the shallows and went in search of more dancing couples. As they worked they quietly sang a fishing song. On the island the herd continued their leisurely search for vegetable ivory; occasionally an elephant would stand in the river to drink.

The mid-afternoon sun started to sink in the sky.

'We should go now Chikomo, while there is still plenty of light for us to see our way home. We have enough fish. Amai and Ambuya will be pleased with our catch.'

As they collected their belongings together, preparing to leave, they glanced across at the island where a young female elephant had found a small patch of mud to wallow in. Amused, they watched her wriggle and roll from side to side, as if in ecstasy. Behind her another young elephant waited her turn; she had been waiting for some time. Finally,

5

she walked down the slope and sat down on her wallowing sister.

The brothers laughed.

'She has become impatient; her sister has taken too long.' said Mahachi.

The back of Baba's old truck was loaded with craftwork from the village. 'Is that everything, Amai?'

'Yes, that is all.'

'Will we see you next week, my son?' asked Ambuya.

'I am not sure. There is something I have to do.'

She nodded.

Baba said goodbye to Ambuya, Amai and his two younger sons and drove out of the village on to the road that ran parallel to the great river. He loved the Zambezi Valley where he had spent his childhood and raised his family. Each time he drove along the wooded route to town he saw something different. Today, swinging from tree to tree, there was a troop of vervet monkeys, with their characteristic bright blue genitals.

When Baba reached town, he delivered the craftwork to the Craft Village and then drove his truck into the car park of the nearby River Hotel, where he was a resident chef.

In the kitchen, chefs were making preparations for the evening meal; the air was beginning to fill with the aromas of cooking. Baba put on his spotless uniform and started to prepare the tiny kapenta fish which were caught in Lake Kariba, further downsteam. He dipped the little fish in flour and fried them in hot oil. When they were cool he put them in small dishes and sent them to the hotel bar, to be served as snacks. Next he collected the ingredients for the bream plaki which he would bake in the oven in a flavoursome sauce using tomatoes, lemon and herbs.

Baba hoped he would not be kept too long in the kitchen tonight. He wanted to be alone in his room, to think.

Later, as he lay in bed, he thought about his forthcoming visit to Dr Meyer. Baba had a sick feeling in the pit of his stomach that the news would not be good. He drifted in and out of a nightmarish sleep. He was glad of the dawn.

His appointment was for twelve noon. He sat waiting nervously in the surgery until his name was called.

'Sit down Baba. How are you feeling?'

'Some days I feel better than others, doctor. I have lost more weight.'

'The results of the tests are not good Baba. I wish you had come to me sooner. There is little I can do for you I'm afraid, except give you drugs to relieve the pain and discomfort.'

'How long do I have?'

'A few months maybe but it is difficult to be precise, Baba.'

Baba's malaise had been with him for more than a year. His visits to the *nganga*, the local witchdoctor, had been of no use. He had anticipated Dr Meyer's news, yet it still left him deeply shocked. Leaving the surgery he made his way to the great river to find solace, stopping for a while by the Devil's Cataract, letting the thunderous noise of the water blot out all thoughts.

Usai, wearing the green uniform of a National Parks Guide, had just finished escorting a group of tourists back to their hotel for lunch when he glimpsed Baba, his father, walking towards The Falls. Something about his father's posture, the way his shoulders were hunched, alarmed Usai and he decided to follow him. He found his father sitting on a fallen tree along the river path, his head buried in his hands. Usai quietly sat down beside him.

'What is it Baba? What has happened?'

Baba's eyes were full of despair as he looked at the face of his beloved first-born.

'How can I begin to tell you, I am so ashamed?' He gazed at the river, silently begging it for courage. 'For many years, I have been drinking at the beer hall during my free time. Sometimes I drank too much and went with one of the women. I have caught a disease ... Doctor Meyer says he cannot help me; I have left it too late. He told me that I have only a short time left before my days end.'

'Oh Baba.' Usai's eyes brimmed with tears which overflowed on to his cheeks. He and Baba sat together for a long while without speaking, both devastated.

Eventually Baba spoke. 'I want to end my time at our village Usai. I would like you to take me home.'

Usai was unable to speak.

'I have taken some leave,' Usai said in a positive voice as he sat at the wheel of Baba's old truck. Usai had shed all his tears in the privacy of his chalet. Baba looked at his son and was glad. He needed someone with strength at his side.

'I would like you to talk to Mahachi and Chikomo for me, explain to them what has happened.'

'Yes of course, Baba.'

As they approached the village he placed his hand on his son's arm. 'Drive slowly Usai, I would like one last look.'

They passed the long island and the Hippo Pool where Baba had learnt to fish when he was a boy and taught Mahachi all his skills. When they reached the old baobab they knew they were almost home.

As they drove into the village they were greeted excitedly by their family. It was several weeks since they had last seen Baba and it was unusual for father and son to visit them at the same time. Baba climbed out of the old truck. There was a sharp intake of breath from Amai; Ambuya grasped her arm, silencing her.

'It is good to see you both,' she said. 'Come and sit in the shade under the tree and take a little food.' Ambuya looked hard at her son, Baba, and observed the dreadful greyness round his mouth, the wasted body. 'While you are eating I will see that your rondavel is as you like it and that your bed is made comfortable.'

'Usai, what is wrong with Baba?' asked Mahachi.

'Let us go into our rondavel,' Usai said to his brothers. 'Baba has asked me to explain what has happened to him.'

Inside, Mahachi and Chikomo sat on the floor listening intently to what Usai had to say.

'Baba has been visiting the beer hall in town. Sometimes he became drunk and slept with other women the way he sleeps with Amai. He should not have done that and he is very ashamed. He has caught a disease from one of them.'

'Did he not go to the *nganga*?' asked Mahachi.

'Yes he did but the *nganga* could not cure him. He also went to the modern doctor but it was too late, he could not help either.'

'Is Baba going to join the spirits?'

'Yes, Chikomo, he is.'

Chikomo and Mahachi sat quietly weeping. Usai watched them, deeply grieved.

That night Mahachi and Chikomo slept close to their older brother, their bodies touching his, drawing comfort from him.

Amai sat with her husband as he dozed on his bed. Although they no longer shared a rondavel, their life together had been good. They had raised a fine family of three sons and two daughters who were now married and living in their husbands' villages, as Amai herself was doing. Baba had looked after her well, she had no complaints. He opened his eyes and they smiled at each other; there was no need for words between them.

'I would like to see Mahachi and Chikomo,' said Baba.

The two boys sat by their father looking down at the diminishing figure that had once seemed so large to them.

Baba's voice was weak when he spoke. 'Mahachi, I have talked to the manager of the River Hotel and told him that you are an excellent fisherman who knows much about the fish in the great river. He asked me if you would be willing to train as a fish chef and take over my position.'

Mahachi turned his head away suddenly and covered his face with his hands.

'I said I would ask you. It is a good job and it would help to support our family. Usai would not be far away from you. Would you be willing?'

'Baba, I am too unhappy to give you an answer at present. I will come back later.'

Baba looked at Chikomo. 'If Mahachi goes away, are you ready to become a fisherman and help feed our family, my son?'

'Yes Baba, I am.'

'Will you learn to go out at night without fear and bring home the cichlids?'

'Yes Baba, I will.'

Life in the village continued as normal. Baba would lie on his bed in the rondavel and listen to the familiar sounds of people going about their daily work. He could hear the sound of children laughing and chattering as they played, he caught the smell of wood smoke and the evening meal simmering. As the days passed, Baba's condition worsened and he became weaker, but still Mahachi had not returned. He spent most of his time in silent contemplation.

'I know what you are thinking Mahachi,' said Chikomo. 'You like being a fisherman and do not want to leave here. But if you work in town, sometimes you will come home for visits and we can still go to the river together, just as we do now. You will always be a fisherman.'

Mahachi considered the shrewd words of his younger brother.

He knelt by Baba's bed as the last rays of the sun shone through the open doorway of the rondavel and lit up the inside. 'I have made my decision Baba, you can rest now and be at peace.'

Baba took Mahachi's hand and pressed it. He watched the sun drop below the horizon, leaving the purple glow of twilight. His eyes closed, finally.

It was early in September when Usai drove out of the village in Baba's old truck with Mahachi at his side. The grass along Zambezi Drive was now parched and yellow. Long dry pods hung from the trees; periodically one would crack open noisily, scattering its seeds onto the ground. The two brothers sat without speaking, each of them deep in thought as they passed the old familiar places.

Usai was reflecting on his close relationship with Baba and how much he would miss their periodic meetings by The Falls, their strolls along the bank of the river when they were both free. He recalled Baba's last words to him: 'You will be the head of our family when I am gone, Usai. Look after them well.'

Mahachi was thinking of his life in the village, the only place he had ever lived. When the time came for him to depart he was reluctant to leave the safety of his childhood sanctuary. That morning he clung to his mother and grand-mother, greatly distressed, until Usai gently led him to the truck.

As he and Usai drove along the road he began to feel nervous and apprehensive about the life that awaited him. 'Baba sometimes talked to me about his work at the hotel but it seemed like another world that did not concern me. Every time I think about living and working there I get a tight feeling in my stomach.'

Usai looked at his younger brother and his expression softened. He could empathise with that feeling, one he himself had once experienced.

'I remember the time when Baba drove me to town to

11

begin my training as a National Parks Guide. "Usai," he said, "there is no need for you to worry, I am sure the people you work with will be helpful and friendly. Look, listen and learn from them and always remember that I will be close by if you need me."'

'Baba said you would not be far away from me, Usai.'

'That is right. Some of my tourists stay at the River Hotel. I will leave messages for you at the reception desk and we can meet when we are both free, just as Baba and I used to do.'

Usai's words greatly comforted Mahachi.

2

Mahachi and Usai walked through the entrance to the River Hotel.

'Good morning, this is Mahachi, Baba's son. He is going to work here,' said Usai to one of the receptionists.

'Good morning, I will tell Mr Jackson that Mahachi is here.'

Usai turned to Mahachi. 'I am going to leave you now, my brother. Remember I will be close by and we shall meet again soon. Do not be afraid, you will be working among Baba's friends.' They shook hands and Mahachi watched as Usai walked out of the door and disappeared. He felt abandoned.

'Mr Jackson is ready to see you now, come this way.' The receptionist took him to a door marked 'Manager' and knocked.

'Come in.'

Mr Jackson walked across the room and shook Mahachi's hand. 'Good morning Mahachi, welcome to the River Hotel. Do sit down.'

'Thank you.' Mahachi sat on a comfortable upright chair facing the manager across his desk.

'We at the hotel were very sorry to hear about Baba, especially the kitchen staff. Baba will be sadly missed, he was a good chef. We are glad to have you, his son, on our staff and hope you will be happy here.'

'I am feeling very nervous.'

The manager smiled; it was a kindly smile. 'No doubt

everything will seem strange to you at first but the kitchen staff are friendly and helpful.' He handed Mahachi a blue folder. 'My secretary has prepared this for you to read. Inside she has explained everything you need to know for the present. Included is a diagram of the hotel so that you will be able to find your way around. You can study the contents of the folder when you have settled in.' He stood up. 'If you go to reception, Everjoy will show you to your room.'

Mahachi collected his holdall from the front entrance where he had left it, and followed Everjoy who talked to him as they climbed a narrow staircase. 'The staff quarters are at the far end of the hotel; your room is on the top floor. You are very lucky, it has a fine view.'

'Usai, my brother, says he will be leaving messages for me at reception.'

'I will see that you receive them as soon as they arrive.' Reaching the end of the stairway, Everjoy turned into a narrow passageway. 'Here is your room, number fifteen.'

Mahachi opened the door and stepped inside. He noticed that the room was small and compact with walls that were painted white. Opposite the door was a window with brightly coloured curtains that matched the cover on the bed. A table and chair stood against the wall to the right and to the left was a wardrobe. There was a small en suite bathroom.

Mahachi put his bag on the floor and walked across to the open window. He leaned out to look at the view. Below was a swimming pool, surrounded by a hedge of bougainvillaea and hibiscus; in front of the hedge were beds of petunias and busy lizzies making a blaze of reds and pinks. Delicate floral fragrances filled the air. A number of people in scant clothing were relaxing beside the pool. Some were lounging on leisure beds, others were sitting on chairs beneath large shady umbrellas.

Although Mahachi had spent his life by the great river, he rarely swam because of the danger of crocodiles and a swift-moving current. Here in the pool people ploughed rhythmically back and forth, in ways that were entirely new to him. Some were swimming on their backs using vigorous strokes; others made gentle rounded movements with their arms. Mahachi watched for a while, fascinated.

His eyes strayed beyond the grounds of the hotel to where he could see a spray cloud rising into the air. He could hear the ever-present rumble of The Falls.

Turning back to look at the room he observed that one of the doors on the wardrobe had a full-length mirror, the first he had ever seen. Sometimes, when he was fishing, Mahachi had caught a glimpse of himself reflected in the river, but this was the first time he had seen a clear reflection of himself.

He walked up to the mirror for a closer look. The face that looked back at him resembled both Usai and his mother, Amai. It was round with small dark eyes, fringed with thick black lashes. His cheeks were high and plump, his nose finely chiselled and his lips clearly defined. He stood farther away from the mirror and turned round slowly, observing himself from all sides. He was tall and his physique was fast approaching manhood. *So this is what I look like,* he thought.

He unpacked his bag and hung his few clothes in the wardrobe. As he was doing so he smiled at his face in the mirror, revealing small, even, white teeth. The face in the glass returned his smile. He grimaced; the reflection grimaced too.

Finally he settled down to read the contents of the folder.

Mid-afternoon, carrying his diagram of the hotel, Mahachi made his way down to the staff dining room to eat. As he passed the kitchen his senses were overpowered by unusual odours that lingered in the air. He was not used to the smell of fried onions and garlic, or the sweet aroma of fruit tarts and cakes baking.

Reaching the dining room door he opened it. People inside were seated at a long table, talking and laughing. One

15

of the men stood up and came towards him smiling, his hand outstretched. '*Masikati* and welcome, you must be Mahachi. I am Mpofu. Come I will show you what to do.' Mahachi was shown to a table where several dishes of food were laid out. 'This is a buffet. You can help yourself to whatever you want. The plates and cutlery are over there.'

Look, listen and learn. Mahachi took a plate and on it he put food that he recognised: fish, vegetables and *sadza*, made from maize meal. He sat down at the table next to Mpofu. He was about to begin eating with his fingers, in the traditional way, when he noticed that Mpofu and the people sitting opposite him were confidently using knives and forks. He returned to the buffet and selected a spoon.

'I worked with your father, Baba, I am also a fish chef,' said Mpofu. 'You and I will be working together when you have finished your training.' Mahachi smiled, delighted. He had taken an instant liking to the man.

That night, Mahachi had difficulty sleeping. Outside his window the sounds were unfamiliar; the clink of glasses and the sound of laughter from the visitors, the occasional splash as someone dived into the pool for a final swim before retiring. His room was so different from the rondavel he shared with Chikomo whose constant chattering he greatly missed. As he lay there, his mind replayed the events of the day. He wished that he could have remained a fisherman but he had made Baba a promise and he had a duty to his family.

At dawn he climbed out of bed and prepared himself for the new day. Before making his way down to the staff dining room for breakfast, he took one last look at himself in the mirror; the reflection looked gloomy.

This morning he was being driven the short distance to the college, in one of the hotel minibuses which was on its way to collect tourists from Victoria Falls Airport. In future Mahachi would be expected to walk to and from the college each day.

16

Inside the college he approached a hatch marked 'Enquiries.' Through it he could see people working at desks. 'Which department are you looking for?' asked one of the staff.

'Catering.'

'Go to your left, it is at the end of the corridor.'

Mahachi followed the directions and walked into a room which was already occupied by other students. He sat down beside a boy of his own age. 'Which hotel do you come from?' ventured Mahachi.

'I am at The Rainbow Inn training to be a pastry chef. What about you?'

'I am living at the River Hotel. I have come here to train as a fish chef.'

Their conversation was interrupted when a man walked into the room and stood facing the group. He was of medium height with a pleasant face and a well-rounded abdomen.

'Good morning students and welcome. My name is Monsieur Boucher and I will be your tutor for the duration of the catering course.'

'Good morning Monsieur Boucher,' said the group in unison.

'I am going to take the register. Perhaps you would be kind enough to raise your hand when I call your name, I may need help with pronunciations.'

Monsieur Boucher perched his ample proportions on the edge of a desk, relaxed with folded arms and addressed the group.

'The course you are taking lasts for six months and your timetable is divided into three main subjects. The first is called Kitchen Hygiene. You will learn about the handling of food and the standards of cleanliness required in the kitchens where you will be working. In the practical part of your work, you will be taught general cooking skills before you specialise in your chosen area. Finally, you will learn about the equipment that is found in hotel kitchens and how it should be used correctly.'

When the group left the college that afternoon they talked non-stop as they walked back to their hotels.

'I have never seen a gas or electric cooker before …'

'Bacteria in the air that are so small we cannot see them …'

'I have seen pastry in a baker's shop in Bulawayo but …'

They were full of enthusiasm for their new-found knowledge, Mahachi no less than the rest. His folder said that after college he was to 'make himself useful' in the hotel kitchen for the rest of the day. He decided to help Mpofu.

'What can I do to help you, Mpofu?' he asked timidly.

'Hello Mahachi, how was your first day?'

'I enjoyed it.'

'That's good. Um, you can help me by preparing the onions and tomatoes for the baked fish.'

Mahachi liked his new routine of attending college in the mornings and helping Mpofu in the afternoons and evenings. He was on his way to the kitchen one afternoon when a note was handed to him by Everjoy at reception. It was from Usai; they were to meet in the hotel car park on Saturday morning.

The two brothers greeted each other warmly. It was their first meeting since Mahachi began his training.

'I am pleased to see you looking so happy, Mahachi. Is your training going well?'

'Yes it is. I am learning a great deal on the catering course and Baba's friends are being very kind to me.'

'That is good news.'

'You said in your message that you needed to talk to me.'

'Yes I do.' Usai had parked his own car next to Baba's old truck. 'When I drove you to the hotel I left the truck here, not sure what to do with it. I think Baba would want you to have it.'

'Would he?' Mahachi's eyes filled with tears. 'A vehicle of my own, I would like that but how will I learn to drive?'

'If you have time to spare we can drive to the Municipal Offices to license the truck in your name and register you as a learner driver.'

'I am not due back at the hotel until this afternoon.'

'So we have plenty of time.'

It took a while to fill in the necessary forms at the office but eventually Mahachi was issued with the appropriate documents and two thick white plastic squares, each with a red letter 'L' in the centre.

'You must tie one to the front of the truck and one to the back,' said Usai, as he drove back to the hotel. 'When we are both free again, I will take you along Zambezi Drive and give you some lessons.'

In the hotel car park they took their leave of each other. Mahachi remained there for sometime admiring the old truck; his truck. He imagined a time when he would be able to drive himself back to the village and visit his family. He would tell them about his life at the hotel and he would also go fishing with Chikomo once more. *Thank you Baba, thank you.*

It was the hottest time of the year; the end of October, 'the suicide month'. The temperature outside was forty degrees Celsius and inside the hotel kitchen it was over fifty. The heat and humidity were making the staff disagreeable, short-tempered and impatient. Perspiration ran down their bodies in rivulets beneath their cotton uniforms. Three cold showers a day gave them only temporary relief. Every window in the kitchen was kept open; the fans hanging from the ceiling were whirling at full speed.

A waiter, who was laying out the hot and cold buffet in the dining room, poked his head through the kitchen hatch. 'Where are the salads I asked for two hours ago,' he exaggerated, 'and when am I going to get the cooked vegetables? The guests will be arriving soon.'

'Isn't the cucumber ready yet, Mahachi?' called Mpofu. 'I cannot wait any longer; I need it to garnish the fish.' A curt reply was on the tip of Mahachi's tongue but he remained silent. He reasoned that soon the rains would come and tempers would cool.

As Mahachi's course progressed, Mpofu encouraged him to practise his skills in the kitchen. At present Mahachi was doing some of the easier tasks such as preparing the garnishes, cleaning and filleting the fish for cooking, and mixing sauces. He paid great attention to the way Mpofu organised his time, watching in awe as he cooked two or three dishes simultaneously, attending to one and then moving to another.

'How do you do it?' Mahachi asked one day when he and Mpofu were sitting together at the table, eating their afternoon meal.

'The menus are always the same, Mahachi. If you pay attention to what I do you will notice that I start some dishes first and leave others until later. Soon you will become accustomed to the routine.'

Mahachi looked forward to a time when he and Mpofu could work as equals.

It was in early November that Mahachi, whose worktop faced the windows, noticed the first large white cumulus clouds appear in the azure sky. Each afternoon more appeared. The horizontal base of the clouds grew darker as they gathered moisture; finally they became black. The kitchen staff peered outside hopefully.

Late in the afternoon Mahachi thought he glimpsed a flash in the sky. He waited. In the distance he heard the faint rumble of thunder; the first storm of the season was marching towards them. Sheet lightning danced across the sky, forked lightning zigzagged towards the earth, a thunderous symphony cracked and rumbled in a final crescendo. Mahachi and other staff paused to watch through the windows.

In the hotel garden a breeze rustled the leaves of the shrubs and cycads. It was followed by a vigorous wind carrying with it the smell of rain falling on sun-baked soil, a rich earthy aroma that heralded growth and renewal.

Outside the kitchen windows the first large globules of water hit the hard, parched ground. Unable to penetrate, they sent tiny puffs of dust up into the air before trickling across the surface. The droplets rapidly became a deluge, the trickle a stream. A dense pounding curtain of rain finally soaked into the flower beds and lawns, drenching them.

From out of unseen holes in the earth flew thousands of minute newly hatched flying ants. They moved towards the lamplight in the road beyond the hotel, fluttering their recently unfolded wings. Beneath the lights people stood waiting with buckets. Mahachi watched, remembering a time when he and his brothers had caught and collected flying ants so that Amai could add them to the other ingredients in her cooking pot.

When the storm had passed, the gardens looked fresh and clean; still and quiet but for the occasional dripping of water off leaves. Cool air blew through the windows into the kitchen, voices were subdued. A new season had begun.

3

Usai's chalet was on the outskirts of town, beyond the shops. Just after dawn he climbed into his car and drove down the long straight road towards the Zambezi. The forest that lined its banks was unusually green and lush, now that the rains had begun. Amid this tropical woodland a faint line of spray rose above the trees. As he drew nearer, the mist became denser and was accompanied by a sound, like a distant earthquake, a rhythmic subterranean rumble: *Mosi-oa-Tunya*, Victoria Falls.

Today was Usai's day off and he had something special planned. He left his car in the car park at the edge of town and walked the short distance to the Victoria Falls Bridge. He went inside the customs shed on the bridge, the border post between Zimbabwe and Zambia. He handed the customs official his visitor's passport.

'How long will you be staying in Zambia?'

'Just one day.'

'What is the purpose of your visit?'

'Tourism.'

His passport was stamped and he began his walk across the bridge, high above the river. He stopped in the centre to look downstream. From his vantage point a spectacular view of arboreal beauty was revealed; a fast-moving river amid steeply wooded banks.

Reaching the end of the bridge he stepped onto Zambian soil and into an area of shady flamboyant trees. Beneath the canopy was a market place where traders were unpacking ebony carvings and men were unlocking small shops which sold cool drinks and bottles of ice-cold beer.

A young man approached Usai, also a National Parks Guide. The two men greeted each other warmly. Their paths had crossed many times and they were well acquainted. They had completed part of their training together.

'*Bwanji* Usai. Welcome to Zambia. It is good to see you.'

'*Bwanji* Maxon. I am glad to meet you again.'

'What brings you here?'

'Some of my tourists have crossed the bridge and seen The Falls from this side. They described the view to me. I wanted to see it for myself.'

'The Falls are at their best during the rains; you have chosen a good time to come. It would be a pleasure to show you the way if you would like some company.'

'I would welcome your company, my friend.'

They walked through the bush in the direction of a tall finger-shaped projection of land. An island pinnacle, eroded and separated from the mainland by the force of water, it could be reached by a footbridge.

'The bridge is only wide enough to take one person. Go ahead, Usai.'

He stepped on to the narrow way and instantly retreated to terra firma. 'It moved!'

'Yes it sways from side to side as you walk but do not worry, it is very strong. The strip and sides are made of metal.'

Treading uncertainly, Usai walked forward. He could feel the movement with each step; he gripped the shoulder-high sides and looked down. 'It is a long way to fall, are you sure this bridge is safe?'

'It is best to keep your eyes fixed on the bushes ahead.'

Usai was relieved when he reached the other side.

'Now we can climb the path to the peak,' said Maxon.

When they reached the top, Usai gazed in wonder at the

panorama before him. There it was, *Mosi-oa-Tunya.* All four sections of it were before him; every breathtaking square inch of it was visible.

Usai was overwhelmed. 'I had no idea it would look like this,' he said.

It looked as though an earthquake had occurred in the far distant past, making a wide crack in the earth, a gorge. The smoothly flowing river spilled its contents over the edge of a precipice and down into the chasm below, before resuming its onward journey.

Usai looked down the full length of the gorge. At the far end, through the mist, he could see the torrent of the Devil's Cataract, like a giant water slide hugging the far bank of the river. In the centre, the Main Falls tipped a gigantic wall of unbroken white-water down into the depths; billowing clouds of mist arose through which rainbows formed and disappeared in the sunlit spray. Closer, rivulets of water spouted out of the rocks. From the mist, arcs of colour reached out from the Rainbow Falls to the miniature rainforest on the opposite side of the gorge.

And there was the noise; the continual unrelenting roar of one million gallons per minute.

Peering over the edge of the peak, Usai saw the swirling water of the Boiling Pot, as it struck the end of the gorge. Twisting and twirling, the current made its way in turmoil on to the river beyond.

'You must be careful Usai, it is very slippery here and there are no rails to hold on to. There have been fatal accidents.'

They stood for a long time, looking at the pulsating heart of the territory in which each of them worked; a vast wilderness which abounded with wildife.

'You are very fortunate, Maxon, to have such a magnificent view of The Falls on this side of the river.'

'And you are lucky to have spent your childhood living in a village by the great river.'

24

'I am reluctant to leave this beautiful place but I am feeling very thirsty. Let us walk back to the market place and I will buy you a Coca Cola or a beer if you prefer,' said Usai.

Under the shadow of the flamboyant trees many more traders had gathered. Usai and Maxon drank chilled Coca Cola as they wandered along the rows of ebony artwork on display.

'Are you looking for anything special? Figures, animals?' asked one of the wood carvers. 'I have many carvings over there. Would you like to take a look?' Usai politely declined.

Turning to Maxon he said, 'I must leave you now, my friend. Thank you for showing me the way.'

'You are welcome.' They shook hands.

Usai walked back across the bridge and into the customs shed where his passport was stamped again.

'Did you enjoy your visit?' enquired the officer.

'Yes very much.'

'Come again.'

The following afternoon, using a National Parks minibus, Usai drove along Zambezi Drive to the A'Zambezi River Lodge on the outskirts of town. He was collecting a group of tourists who wished to be escorted around The Falls. He took them first to a large bronze statue of David Livingstone which stood in the centre of the path leading to the Devil's Cataract.

'Many people believe that David Livingstone discovered these falls because he named them after his queen – Victoria. But he was the first white man to see them. Local people who live along the Zambezi Valley have always known about them. Their name for The Falls is *Mosi-oa-Tunya*; the smoke that thunders.'

'How did David Livingstone discover them?'

'It is said that he and his bearers were travelling at dusk in canoes when they heard a very loud noise ahead of them. It was too dark to see what was there, so Livingstone decided to break his journey and set up camp. The following morning this is what he found.'

'Where did he make camp?'

'The island in the river behind the centre of The Falls is called Livingstone Island and that is where he camped for the night, it is told.'

'So he had no idea of the danger nearby?'

'No he did not.'

Usai led the group of tourists at a leisurely pace through the small rainforest created by the warm spray that drifted in waves across the gorge. Everything was damp, the air humid. Liana vines hung down like long ropes; on the ground, there were groups of unusual fungi and red puffball-shaped flowers were blooming.

Stopping at the many viewing points throughout the rainforest, Usai gave the group time to gaze at different parts of The Falls. He stood quietly by as they took photographs and were soon drenched by the mist.

'If you would like to do some shopping I can show you the Craft Village,' said Usai at the end of their tour. 'It is close by in a square, on Main Street.' The group was very keen to see the village.

'The rondavel on the left,' said Usai, as he led them through the village, 'belongs to the *nganga*, the witchdoctor. He provides people with traditional medicines.' The group walked on. 'The stone carvings in this shop are made from soapstone or serpentine. You can see that the shop opposite specialises in wood carvings. At the far end of the village women are selling crochet work.' Many dainty duchesse sets and large tablecloths were hanging from a wall, making a fine display. 'I will leave you to browse; there are many things of interest to look at and buy.'

'Are we permitted inside the *nganga's* rondavel?'

'Yes, of course. He will show you the plants he uses to make his medicines, but he will expect to be paid.'

It was almost sundown when Usai and his tourists climbed into the minibus to travel back to their hotel. As they approached the A'Zambezi River Lodge, Usai saw that the front door was open wide and the foyer filled with light. Through a window, he could see people sitting at the bar drinking 'sundowners'.

A movement on the road ahead startled him. He stopped the vehicle. 'Look in front of the bus,' he whispered to the tourists.

They watched as a pride of lions padded slowly across the road, pausing a few feet from the open door of the hotel to sniff the air before continuing on their way through the bush and down to the river to drink.

There was just one small shopping centre in the town of Victoria Falls, on Main Street. On the corner of the block was a coffee bar, a gathering place for those who worked locally and the only place in town where young African girls could go without a chaperone. Further along Main Street there was a chemist shop and a supermarket.

The street looked clean, washed by a heavy downpour of rain, when Usai took a trolley and walked into the super-market. The young woman at the checkout point saw him come in and her eyes followed him as he moved along the aisles and finally arrived at her till. They smiled at each other.

'Hello Chipo, are you well?'

'Hello Usai, yes I am fine. It is a while since I last saw you at the coffee bar.'

'I rarely find the time to go there during the day.'

She watched as he wheeled the trolley to his car and loaded his shopping into the boot. They waved goodbye to each other as he drove off.

Chipo was a pretty young woman; she and Usai used to meet briefly at the coffee bar during their lunch breaks, to sit drinking cold milk shakes and talk about their lives and families. In her daydreams, Chipo imagined that one day her father would be approached and she would become part of Usai's family.

'It is time you were married,' Baba had once said to Usai. 'Chipo will make you a good wife. She will bear you many children.' Baba had been thinking of her fine child-bearing hips.

Usai had been about to ask Baba to begin marriage negotiations when Baba had died. Afterwards, Usai's interest in Chipo began to wane. By the start of the rainy season they saw each other only by chance or at the supermarket. Nelisiwe – Neli – had come into Usai's life.

It was at the end of a busy day that Usai, on his way down Main Street, noticed a tall young woman walking ahead of him. Her well-rounded buttocks rotated rhythmically as she moved. She went into the coffee bar, collected a cool drink and sat down next to the window, gazing out at the passing traffic.

Following her, Usai went to the counter and ordered a milkshake. The coffee bar was quite full so he had an excuse to sit at the vacant seat opposite her. She glanced at him as he sat down, then turned her head and continued to look out of the window. He noticed that her large brown eyes were set in a beautiful oval face.

Sneaking several sidelong glances at her as he sipped his drink, he finally summoned the courage to speak to her. 'I have not seen you in here before. Do you work in town?'

She looked at him. 'Yes I have recently started work at the chemist shop. I come here sometimes for a cool drink while I am waiting for my bus. There is only one an hour.'

Encouraged, Usai continued. 'Which bus do you take?'

'I take the number twenty-six, the one to the Eastern Township.'

'Oh. My name is Usai by the way.'

'Mine is Nelisiwe, Neli.'

They smiled at each other.

Suddenly she stood up. 'There is my bus. I must go.' She hurried outside, ran across the road and stepped onto the bus that had stopped by the kerb.

After that Usai found any excuse to walk past the chemist shop to catch a glimpse of her. Whenever possible he would try to be nearby when the shop closed for the day, so that he could follow her at a discreet distance, to see if she went into the coffee bar. On the occasions when she did, he would sit opposite her so that they could talk.

'When we first met you were wearing the uniform of a guide.'

'Yes. At present I escort tourists around The Falls.'

'I have heard that the training is long.'

'Yes it is. A guide is expected to study all the flora and fauna in the area where he intends to work. Do you enjoy watching wildlife?'

'I have no interest in animals and birds but since working at the chemist shop I have become interested in modern medicine.'

'Do you not use the *nganga*?'

'Sometimes, but I have been studying the products sold in the shop and the illnesses they cure. I think some of them are better than the *nganga*.'

'Those are very strong opinions.' He smiled, amused by her comments.

As they grew more comfortable in each other's company they took walks to The Falls or along the river path. Occasionally Neli made disparaging remarks regarding the old traditions but Usai did not take them seriously.

One afternoon as Neli emerged from the shop, Usai was waiting for her. She hurried towards him, smiling. 'Hello Usai.'

As he stood looking at her, he realised how strong his feelings for her had become. It was time to send a member of his family to begin the long slow marriage negotiations with her father.

'Come, let us walk by the river, I want to talk to you.' They sat down on a seat by the river path. Usai longed to touch her intimately but it was taboo; he must wait. 'I would like us to be married, Neli. On my next day off I shall go to my village and speak to Baba's brother, Little Father. He will negotiate for me. When a *lobola* has been agreed, you and I can discuss when to hold our marriage at the village.'

'But Usai, we are urban dwellers and these are modern times. Once you have agreed on the *lobola* we could marry soon afterwards, at the Registry Office in town.'

He looked at her, shocked. 'Surely you are not suggesting we forget our marriage customs? My family would expect a traditional ceremony and a feast.'

Neli did not reply.

Usai was silent for a while. When he spoke it was with determination.

'I want us to be married in my village.'

4

Little Father was sitting on a stool outside his rondavel in the village. Using a knife he was skilfully carving the head of a man out of a piece of wood. He did not notice Usai approach. Usai stood watching him for a while, observing Little Father's close resemblance to Baba.

'*Mangwanani* Little Father. That is a fine carving,' said Usai at length.

'*Mangwanini* Usai, I did not see you there.' He smiled; Baba's smile. 'I hope it will fetch a good price when it is sold at the Craft Village. Sit down beside me and tell me your news.' Little Father listened attentively as Usai spoke about his recent activities and reported on Mahachi's new life at the hotel.

'I will pass your news on to others; they will be glad to hear it.'

'I need your help, Little Father.'

'What is it?'

'There is a young woman I have become fond of. Nelisiwe, Neli. I want her to become my wife. I would like you to negotiate for me.'

The old man smiled. 'I would be glad to. Tell me about the young woman.'

Usai told him how they had met and where Neli lived and worked.

'Did Baba like her?'

'Baba did not meet her.'

31

'Do you think he would have liked her, had they met?'

'I do not know, Little Father. Neli does not always share my views on the old customs. She wants to be married at the Registry Office in town.'

'That would not be suitable Usai, it is not our way.'

'I know Little Father and it is not my wish. I want a traditional ceremony here in our village.'

'I must discuss this with Neli's father when we meet.'

'Will you come with me when I return to town tomorrow?'

'Yes I will. Now you must speak to Amai and Ambuya. It is expected.'

Usai's conversation with his mother and grandmother did not go well. At first they laughed with joy when he told them he had spoken to Little Father.

'So at last you are going to marry Chipo, my son. It was Baba's wish. He told us that she came from a village to the south and she would understand our ways. I am so happy. Soon I will have grandchildren.'

'Amai, it is not Chipo I intend to marry.' He said the words softly, knowing they would shock.

'Not Chipo?'

'No Amai. Her name is Nelisiwe, Neli.'

'Baba did not tell us about her.'

'They did not meet.'

'You are going to marry someone unknown to the family? Come, sit down beside me, my son, and tell me about Neli.'

Amai and Ambuya did not like what they heard. 'There are women in the village with sons who have married young women from the township. They have encountered many problems,' said Ambuya.

Usai did not comment.

In a house in the Eastern Township, Little Father and Khumalo, Neli's father, stood facing each other. Khumalo was a tall dignified man, dressed in the smart clothing of an

32

urban dweller. The two men greeted each other and shook hands.

'Sit down Little Father.'

'Thank you Khumalo.' Little Father chose a comfortable armchair; Khumalo sat opposite him.

'My daughter has told me that she wishes to marry Usai but she wants to be married at the Registry Office. She would like a marriage certificate and birth certificates for her children, in the modern way. She does not want her family to carry identity cards, as those of us who were born in rural areas do. She shares the view of many young people in the township.'

'I know this. The ways of the young are not always our ways, but Usai would not agree to such a marriage. His mother and grandmother would refuse to attend. They expect a traditional ceremony in their village.' Little Father looked at Khumalo. 'Surely, you as her father can persuade Neli to change her mind?'

'My daughter makes a generous financial contribution to our family; I feel obliged to consider her views. But there is a way, perhaps, that the wishes of all might be satisfied.'

'How is that possible?'

'After the *lobola* has been agreed, a small civil ceremony could be held with Usai, Neli and ourselves. Later, there could be a large traditional marriage and feast at the village, when both our families would be present. Honour would be satisfied on both sides, I think.'

'I will deliver your suggestion to Usai and return with him in two weeks so that we can further our discussions.'

Usai was waiting outside in his car. As he drove back to town he listened carefully to everything Little Father had to say.

'What is your opinion, Little Father?'

'If you wish to have a traditional ceremony and no other you must choose a different wife, one who shares our belief in the old customs. If you insist on marrying Neli you will have to compromise. It is for you to decide, Usai.'

They sat without speaking; Little Father waited. In his heart he knew what Usai would decide and it saddened him.

'I love Neli and want to marry her. I accept Khumalo's proposal.'

'My village is in the south beyond the tsetse fly zone. I expect the *lobola* to be paid in cattle which will be added to the family herd.' Khumalo was speaking to Usai; Little Father was at his side.

'How many head of cattle would you expect?'

'My daughter is well educated and she has a good job which will bring money into your household, money that I can no longer depend on. I would expect twenty-five head of cattle.'

Usai had not anticipated a payment in cattle; he was expecting to pay in goats. The demand was excessive and Usai knew that he must barter.

'There are no cattle hereabouts to buy, therefore I would need to make a journey south to purchase them. Also, I understand that the civil ceremony requires a fee. I could afford no more than fifteen head of cattle.'

'I will accept no fewer than twenty.'

They settled on eighteen, to be paid over an unspecified period. Usai would have them sent to Khumalo's village in the south.

Usai drove Little Father back to the village. He had not spoken since they had left town. As they approached the old baobab tree he said, 'I am not accustomed to modern marriages Usai. I think Mahachi should accompany you to the civil ceremony in my place.'

5

Chikomo stepped outside his rondavel and looked around the village, stretching his arms and yawning as he did so. It was mid-afternoon and he had spent the day sleeping, after a night of fishing. He noticed the large thorny *bomas* were still open and empty. Soon the older boys would be returning with the goat herds; enclosed for the night in their prickly pens the animals would be safe from carnivores.

He could see Amai and Ambuya with the village women, working in the fields. His eyes wandered away from the large cultivated enclosure to an oblong area of bare earth near the dirt road; the football field. At each end of it there stood a structure. Using flexible green twigs, skilfully woven in the manner of basketry, two undersized, irregular-shaped goals had been fashioned.

Some small boys were on the field kicking a ball; Chikomo ambled towards them. He enjoyed teaching the boys to dribble and tackle, pass and score goals. When they were not attending the rural school or doing their tasks, the boys would use every spare moment to practise the skills Chikomo had taught them.

'Hey Chikomo, come and join us.'

'Show us some of your tricks,' said Pita, the smallest boy.

The group watched as Chikomo balanced the football on top of his foot and tossed it up and down several times, without letting it fall to the ground. Then he expertly dribbled the ball down the length of the football field and kicked it into goal. The boys laughed and applauded. They adored Chikomo, especially Pita.

Glancing across the dirt road that bordered the village, Chikomo observed that part of the cordon sanitaire had been trampled. *Probably an elephant*, he thought. Within the cordon was a minefield, a reminder of the *Chimurenga*, the Liberation Struggle that had ended five years ago, in 1980. Chikomo made a mental note to report the damage to the village elders but at that moment he heard a car approaching. Recognising the sound of the engine he raced to the entrance of the village, all thought of the breach in the fence forgotten. Usai had come to visit them.

When Usai brought the news that he and Neli were betrothed, Chikomo expected Amai to show more pleasure. She was pleased but Chikomo sensed that something was wrong. He tried to engage her in conversation. 'You are not smiling as much as I expected Amai ...'

'Not smiling?'

'... for a mother who's eldest son is soon to be married and provide her with grandchildren.'

Amai was evasive. 'I am very busy at present; there is much work to do in the fields.'

'Are you displeased because Neli was not Baba's choice?'

'Chikomo, I will talk to you when I am ready.'

He spoke to Ambuya and Little Father. 'Why is Amai not overjoyed that Usai is betrothed?'

Their replies were the same. 'You must ask her.'

'I have asked her,' said Chikomo angrily. 'She is not ready to tell me. Surely I should be told; Usai is my brother.'

Around the village Chikomo started to hear Usai's name mentioned in hushed tones. He began to eavesdrop. He learnt that after the marriage Neli would not be living in the village with them, as was the custom. His curiosity grew.

One afternoon he heard the raised voices of women,

gossiping in the fields as they worked. He walked in their direction hoping to hear what they were saying.

Close by, some boys were playing in the football field. One of them called out to him. 'Come and play, Chikomo, we need one more person to make a team.'

Pita ran towards him and took his hand. 'I want to be in your team, Chikomo.'

The boys began to play a game of five-a-side football. As he played, Chikomo strained his ears to catch any stray words that floated across from the women nearby.

'... two ceremonies ...'

'... together in Usai's chalet before the traditional ...'

Chikomo tried to piece the fragments of conversation together. He was not concentrating on the game. Somebody kicked the ball in his direction; he dribbled it down the field and attempted to score a goal. It was a mighty kick rooted in resentment.

The ball rose above the goalpost, travelled across the dirt road and through the breach in the cordon sanitaire. Pita ran swiftly after the ball to retrieve it, before any of the boys could warn him of the danger.

The explosion was deafening. In a frozen moment of horror Chikomo watched as Pita's little body was hurled into the air and landed in the long grass. Chikomo raced towards the fence.

'No! No!'

A hush fell over the entire village. The women in the fields stopped working and stood like a silent tableau, their eyes turned towards the minefield. Even the birds ceased their singing.

Chikomo stood by the opening, sobbing; no sound reached him from the long grass. Not even a whisper or childlike whimper.

Suddenly the boys were running towards the cordon, crying and shouting. Men and women ran after them; they gathered around the breach craning their necks in an effort to identify the victim.

'Pita is in there,' cried Chikomo, covering his face with his hands.

'Who did he say?'

'It is Pita.'

'Pita!'

Pita's family wailed and screamed at the mention of his name; Ina, his mother collapsed on the ground, weeping hysterically. Relatives rushed to her side, enclosing her in their comforting arms. Screaming and crying she tore herself away from them in an attempt to reach her beloved child. They clung to her, pulling her back to the safety of the dirt road.

The crowd could hear the sound of an approaching helicopter on regular border patrol, drawn to the sound of the explosion. Coming into view as it cleared the tops of the nearby trees, it hovered above the minefield. Looking up, Chikomo could see a man standing by the open door. A winch was attached to him and he was lowered to the place where Pita had landed. As the man and child were slowly raised, Chikomo could see Pita's life-blood spurting from the place where his legs had been.

Amai sat up, startled out of her sleep. There it was again, the groaning and crying. She crept into Chikomo's rondavel and sat beside him. Ambuya joined her. Chikomo was asleep yet his body was tossing and turning; the sounds he made were those of someone in torment. The two women sat with him until he became quiet, then they returned to their own rondavels.

In the morning, Amai and Ambuya watched Chikomo set off for the river.

'He is not eating, see how thin he is getting.'

'His walk used to be proud and upright, now he stoops.'

'Look at his face, it is full of fear. He rarely speaks yet his lips are moving silently and rapidly, talking to the unseen.'

'I will search my store of *muti* for something to help him sleep undisturbed.'

'I do not think your medicine will be enough Ambuya, his sickness is of the mind.'

'You think the spirits are tormenting him?'

'I am not sure. The other boys were troubled by what they saw yet they are not getting thinner, they do not cry out in their sleep.'

Amai spent the day pondering a solution. 'Chikomo is my youngest child,' she mumbled to herself as she went about her work, 'I will have no more children now that Baba has passed into the spirit world. I cannot remain idle while my son wastes away.'

'Chikomo you are unwell. I see that something is troubling you, tell me what it is.' Chikomo sat in silence, not wishing to speak. 'Tell me, my son.'

'It was my fault that Pita died, Amai.'

'Why do you say that?'

'I saw the breach in the fence and forgot to report it to the elders.' Tears trickled down his cheeks. 'It was I who kicked the football into the minefield. The spirits are angry with me, I see them in my dreams.'

Amai now understood the magnitude of her dilemma. She did not speak for some time after Chikomo's confession, she sat deep in thought. She knew that she ought to take him to the *nganga*, who would perform a ritual and make offerings of appeasement, but if people learnt that the spirits were angry with Chikomo their family might be driven out of the village. At the very least, Chikomo would be sent an evil token, a *tokoloshe*. *I must find a way to ease your suffering, my son*, she thought.

'Come with me,' said Amai gently. She walked out of the

village and on to the deserted dirt road. Chikomo trailed behind her at a distance, his head bowed. Suddenly he stopped, recognising a landmark. They were walking towards the cordon.

'No Amai. No! I cannot go there,' he cried fearfully. He slumped to his knees, sobbing in anguish. Amai rushed back to him. 'I cannot go that way, the spirits may be waiting.'

She enfolded her son in her arms to comfort him. 'Hush.' She spoke in a quiet soothing voice, 'I am going to the cordon to speak to Pita. I want to tell him how sad I am that he has left us and hope he is happy in his spirit world. I do not think the spirits will be angry if you come with me and tell Pita that you are sorry.'

Amai stood up and walked slowly on. When she reached the minefield she closed her eyes. Remembering that dreadful day she whispered words of regret, sorrow and appeasement. Without opening her eyes, she sensed that Chikomo was beside her.

'What shall I say, Amai?'

'You must say what is in your heart, Chikomo. Speak the truth.'

He wiped his tear-stained face with the back of his hand and raised his eyes. Fixing them on the place where Pita had fallen, he began to speak hesitantly.

'I forgot ... I forgot to tell them about the broken fence.' The tears were beginning again. 'I kicked the ball too high.' He burst into uncontrollable weeping.

'Have courage, my son.'

'I did not mean to hurt you Pita,' he said between sobs. 'I am very sorry ... please forgive me ... I miss you. I wanted to take you fishing one day.'

Amai put her arm round Chikomo's shoulders and pulled him close. Mother and son stood for a while without speaking.

A colourful bird, the size of a dove, flew out of the trees

and perched on top of the newly mended fence, in front of them. Its body was reddish-brown; the brown tail was in contrast to the blue-grey wings. Its black head was encircled with a band of white. It was a Heughlin's robin, the totem of their people. When it opened its beak the long melodious song that came from its throat was the most beautiful they had ever heard. They listened enraptured. Even after the last note was silent, the song lingered on in their minds. Suddenly the robin flew back into the trees.

'I think that was a sign, Chikomo.'

'A sign?'

'Yes. There were words in that happy joyous song even though we could not understand them; a message.'

'A message from Pita?'

'Yes, I think so.'

'Telling us that he is happy in his spirit home and that he is not angry with me?'

'Yes. That is what I believe.'

Chikomo turned a bright smiling face towards his mother. It was a long time since she had seen that smile which reminded her so much of Baba. Chikomo's face slowly crumpled as he wept, his large brown eyes releasing tears of relief.

6

'Can I come with you today, Chikomo?' She looked at him,
her face open and guileless.

'Girls do not go fishing, Tabeth.'

'I do not want to fish; I have to look after our baby while my
mother is working. I want to walk with you to the pools and
watch you. I will not hinder you, Chikomo, I will sit quietly on
the river bank.'

'Hm. I usually go alone, it is what I prefer, but I suppose it
will do no harm just this once. You must promise not to
bother me while I work, Tabeth.'

'I promise, Chikomo.'

They walked together along the dirt road and down to the
pools, Chikomo carrying his fishing equipment, Tabeth
holding a plastic bag with enough food for the three of them.
On her back the child was sleeping.

Although small in stature, Tabeth was the same age as
Chikomo. They had attended the rural school together and
would soon be young adults. She and Chikomo used to be
friends but now he avoided her, for Tabeth was Pita's sister.
Although Chikomo was no longer troubled by spirits and had
regained his former strength, he knew that he had wronged
Pita's family and Tabeth's presence reminded him of this.

Tabeth sat in the shade, watching Chikomo as he stood in
the shallows waiting for the spawning bream to exhaust
themselves. The child began to cry. Tabeth removed the baby
from her back and spread on the ground the large towel that

42

enclosed it. She fed the infant a little mealie meal porridge and gave it some water to drink. Afterwards she played with the child until it became sleepy again.

'The fishing is slow today,' mumbled Chikomo. 'I have caught only three so far.' He walked to the bank and sat down on the towel beside Tabeth. She untied the bag of food and handed Chikomo a cold mealie meal fritter, made from leftover *sadza*. She took one for herself. The sleeping child lay beside them.

'I miss Pita,' Tabeth remarked in a soft voice. 'Sometimes I carried him on my back, when he was a baby. I was still small myself and he seemed very heavy to me. Pita liked you very much, Chikomo, he often talked about you. Your company helps to lessen my sadness.'

'I miss him too, Tabeth.' Chikomo looked at her and noticed a tear roll down her cheek onto her dress; he was ashamed. 'Do not cry, Tabeth.'

'I cannot help it.'

Chikomo stood up and walked back into the river.

During the afternoon, he glanced at her from time to time. When their eyes met he turned away.

'I have enough fish now, Tabeth, we should leave soon.' He began threading the fish he had caught onto a length of wire, watching Tabeth as he did so.

'We must go now little one,' she said, kneeling beside the infant. Picking up the towel she tied two ends of it tightly at the front of her waist. The other two ends she pulled up underneath her arms and put them into her mouth. With a twist and a turn she swung the tiny infant by its arms over her head, and bending forward placed the baby inside the fold. She pulled the towel tightly under her arms and tied the loose ends firmly across the top of her chest. Chikomo smiled as he watched her small hands checking the bundle on her back, making sure that the baby was secure before rising to her feet.

They walked slowly back to the village, Chikomo with his fish threaded in a neat row on the piece of wire which dangled at his side, Tabeth carrying the child on her back.

'I have enjoyed your company today, Chikomo. Will you let me come with you again sometimes?'

'I prefer to fish on my own, unless I am with Mahachi.' Seeing the look of disappointment on her face he added quickly, 'But I will think about it, Tabeth.'

When they reached the village they went their separate ways. Amai was waiting for Chikomo outside his rondavel. She seemed agitated.

'I see that Tabeth accompanied you today, Chikomo.'

'Yes Amai, she is still sad at the loss of Pita and I was his friend. She wanted my company.'

'I understand that, my son, but an unguarded word from you, repeated by Tabeth to her mother, might harm our family. We could still be driven out of the village.'

'I know, Amai, but I said nothing to Tabeth that I regret, nor will I in the future.'

Amai looked relieved. 'That is good to know, my son.'

'Tabeth asked if she could come with me again.'

'I do not think it would be wise, and besides you must remember that soon you will be a young man and Tabeth a maiden. When that happens you will not be permitted to be alone together.' She smiled at her son, knowing how much he longed to be a man like his brothers.

Chikomo decided not to take Tabeth with him again.

After his meeting with Tabeth and her reminder of his troubled times, Chikomo's commitment to the village changed. He had taken his life there for granted, believing that he would live in the village forever, as his ancestors had done. But his single act of forgetfulness, and the effect it might have had on his family, diminished his sense of security.

He decided to put aside his childish pursuits, and when he was not fishing he would use his free time to learn the skills that he needed as an adult; skills that would contribute to the traditions of the community and make him a respected member of it.

Chikomo noticed that preparations were being made to build a new rondavel. He watched as a site was selected and an area of bush cleared. He knew that it would take months to complete the work and it was this that prompted him to leave the entertainment of the children to others and join the men out in the forest, felling the *mdondo* trees that would be used to form the structure of the rondavel.

In the weeks that followed, a small figure could be seen among the grown men, helping to carry the felled trees back to the village and stack them at the clearing.

'Come and sit with us Chikomo. I will show you what to do next,' said one of the young men. 'Do you have a good sharp knife?'

'Yes I have this one; it belonged to Baba.'

'It is a fine knife. Now, this is what you do. Take your knife and carefully remove strips of bark from the trees, like so. You must put the strips over there,' he said, pointing. 'They will be used later for binding.'

The *mdondo* trees, once devoid of bark, were sawn into poles of equal length by skilled carpenters. Chikomo watched as the poles were driven into the ground to form a circle, the foundation of the wall.

'It is very important for the rondavel to be strong and long lasting, Chikomo. It must withstand torrential rain and seasonal storms, as well as fierce sunlight and parching.' Chikomo listened attentively to the carpenter, eager to learn as much as possible.

Amai was pleased. 'There was a time,' she said to Ambuya one day, 'when I feared that Chikomo would decide to join his brothers in the town, and I would be left here, all my sons and daughters gone. But now I think Chikomo will spend the rest of his life in the village.'

At mealtimes when he was ravenous from the exertions of manual labour they gave him extra large portions of food, listening as he spoke with enthusiasm about each stage of the construction.

'What have you been doing today, Chikomo?' asked Amai, as Ambuya heaped food onto his plate.

'We have been working on the wall, Amai. The men have begun to place saplings in between the poles. I have been using strips of bark to bind the saplings and poles together, to hold them securely in place.' He chewed and swallowed a large mouthful of food before continuing. 'Later I went to the clearing to watch some of the carpenters working on the roof poles, shaving and whittling the ends so that they will fit closely together, to form the point of the roof.'

Amai and Ambuya smiled and nodded.

In spite of Chikomo's decision not to take Tabeth fishing, she was still eager for his company. Chikomo noticed that their paths crossed more often than they used to around the village. When he returned from fishing he would find her waiting by the village entrance. 'Have you caught many fish today, Chikomo?' she would ask, as she walked with him to the cooking area.

At the building site he would sometimes turn and see her standing nearby, watching him. Little Father commented one day. 'Chikomo, I have noticed that Tabeth is showing an interest in you. Her eyes follow you and she seeks you out. You are both still young but she is a modest girl and in time she will make a good wife.'

'I am not interested in girls, Little Father. I am too busy.'

Little Father chuckled.

As the rondavel grew, so did Chikomo. His slim childish body began to transform and he noticed the first signs of manhood. It was at the end of a busy week that he realised he had not seen Tabeth for some days. 'Amai, it is a while since I last saw Tabeth. Has something happened to her?'

46

'Yes indeed, my son, it has. Tabeth has become a maiden. You will no longer see her alone; she will be in the company of other maidens.'

Chikomo was surprised by his own feelings. He was disappointed that Tabeth would not be waiting for him at the village entrance when he returned from fishing, that their paths would no longer cross as they used to.

7

On the edge of town was the railway line. The booms were down across Main Street, barring the way to pedestrians and traffic. Mahachi stood waiting as the daily steam train moved between the booms and pulled slowly into the station, the terminus of the Bulawayo to Victoria Falls line. The train stopped with a jerk and a series of clanks. Doors were flung noisily open and people disembarked; mail and provisions for the shops and hotels were unloaded.

Mahachi watched as suntanned backpackers emerged, carrying their copies of the *Lonely Planet* guide book. He knew they would stay in the municipal chalets and lodges which could be rented for a few American dollars a night. Since moving to the hotel, Mahachi had become interested in the tourists who visited the town; their appearance, the different languages they spoke and the food they preferred. He himself had long since ceased to eat only traditional food.

After the booms were raised Mahachi walked the short distance to the path that led into the small rainforest. This afternoon Usai was due to give him another driving lesson. The note left at reception said that they were to meet by The Falls. It was a while since their last meeting and Mahachi was particularly looking forward to hearing news of Usai's marriage negotiations.

He located his brother with some tourists viewing the Main Falls and Livingstone Island. He sat on a nearby bench waiting for Usai to finish with his group. The dripping trees in the forest made the air hot and humid; feeling lethargic, Mahachi started to doze.

'*Masikati* Mahachi. Have you fallen asleep?' It was Usai's voice.

Mahachi opened his eyes and smiled at his brother. 'Yes I must have.' He stood up. '*Masikati* my brother, and how are your marriage negotiations progressing?'

'I must talk to you about them before we start the driving lesson. Let us go and sit in the truck.'

As they walked along the narrow path a young tourist brushed past Mahachi; her fine smooth hair, which hung to her waist, trailed along his arm. Its soft silkiness surprised him and he felt himself stir. His eyes followed her until she disappeared from view.

Sitting inside the vehicle Mahachi said, 'Tell me your news, Usai.'

'My marriage negotiations are now complete; I am betrothed.'

'Congratulations! That is very good news. You are going to marry Chipo at last, Amai will be so pleased. It was ...'

Usai cut him short. 'I will not be marrying Chipo. I am going to marry Nelisiwe, Neli. She is the young woman who works at the chemist shop on Main Street.'

Mahachi frowned, confused. 'When you told me you had approached Little Father I thought ... Baba always talked about Chipo; I assumed you would be marrying her.'

'I intended to once, it was Baba's wish, but after he died I met Neli.'

'Oh.' Mahachi said nothing further. It was not his place to question the decisions of his older brother.

'Let me explain my marriage plans. First of all, we are going to be married at the Registry Office, and later in the year there will be a traditional marriage.'

'You are going to have two marriages; one in town and another in the village?' Mahachi was shocked. 'But why?'

49

'Neli is an urban dweller, she was born in the township and her views are modern; she does not believe in some of the old customs. I have compromised for her sake.'

Mahachi sat quietly, trying to absorb the details of such a strange arrangement.

Usai continued, 'Mahachi, I need you to accompany me to the civil ceremony in town, to be my witness and to sign some papers. Little Father does not want to do it.'

'When will the ceremony take place and who will be there?'

'The marriage will be conducted at the end of May, after the rains have finished and the weather is cooler. There will be just four of us.'

'So few people. So there will be no celebration afterwards?'

'No.'

'You will have to tell me what to do, Usai, I know nothing of town marriages but I will gladly be your witness.' He smiled suddenly and embraced Usai. 'I wish you much happiness, my brother, even though your news was unexpected.'

'Thank you Mahachi.'

'Now can we begin the driving lesson? I would like to pass my driving test soon so that I can visit the village. I want to see Amai and Ambuya again and go fishing with Chikomo.'

Later, Mahachi and Mpofu were working side by side in the kitchen. 'How was your driving lesson today, Mahachi?' Mpofu asked.

'It went well. Usai says I am ready to book a driving test.' Mahachi thought about his conversation with Usai. 'Where were you married, Mpofu?'

'At the Registry Office in town. Afterwards we had a celebration at the Community Centre in the township. Why are you asking? Are you thinking of getting married? Hey everyone! Mahachi is getting married.'

Several of the staff laughed. 'You have kept it very quiet,

Mahachi,' said the pastry chef. 'It is easy to see what a fine handsome man you have become, now that you are eating our food, but do you have enough money for the *lobola*?'

Mahachi giggled with embarrassment. 'No, no I am not the one. It is my brother Usai who is getting married. I am to be his witness.'

'Will you be having a big celebration afterwards?' enquired Mpofu.

'No. There will be only four of us.'

'Hm. I suppose you cannot celebrate with just four people although … there might be a way…'

'What do you mean?'

'Now that you have completed your training and are receiving a salary, you could speak to Mr Jackson, the manager. He might allow the four of you to have a meal together in the dining room, after the ceremony. Each month, he will deduct some of the cost from your wages, until the full amount is paid.'

'I will speak to Everjoy at reception and ask to see the manager.'

Mahachi walked along the hotel drive beneath the flamboyant trees; their vermilion flower clusters were surrounded by finger-like leaves which formed a shady canopy. When he reached Main Street he struggled through the barrier of searing heat that reflected off the unshaded pavement. He was glad to reach the Municipal Building and the cooling fans rotating on the ceiling.

'I have come to book a driving test,' Mahachi said to the official at the desk.

He was handed some forms. 'If you would like to fill these in and bring them back to me …'

Sitting down at a nearby table, Mahachi completed the task. 'Your test will be two weeks from today,' said the official.

Mahachi decided to take the longer route back to the

hotel. He crossed to the other side of Main Street, where the shopkeepers had pulled awnings over the pavement to shade their shops and keep them cool. He looked through the window of the chemist shop and saw that a young woman was serving a customer. *So that is Neli.* He watched her for a while unnoticed. She looked quite different from the young women in the village; there was no dust on her face or clothing, from her labours. The crisp whiteness of the spotless overall she wore gave her a sterile appearance. She moved quickly and efficiently about the shop, smiling confidently as she served the customers.

He tried to imagine her working with Amai, but he could not.

8

Mahachi set off at dawn in Baba's old truck. As he drove alone along Zambezi Drive he was excited by the prospect of seeing his family after such a long absence. Beyond the perimeter of the town he noticed that the forest was dense with new foliage; the previously parched earth he had left behind in September was now a thick green carpet. Close to the great river, small groups of waterbuck were grazing on the verdant banks. Male kudus with magnificent spiral horns were browsing on the fresh leaves of bushes and shrubs.

Suddenly, through the trees, he glimpsed them at last; the long island and the Hippo Pool. He stopped for a while to gaze once again at the place where he had expected to spend the rest of his life. He breathed deeply, inhaling the scent of familiar plants and feeding herbivores, so different from the smells he had recently become accustomed to in the kitchen.

He drove on, overtaking some women who were walking towards the village with bundles of firewood balanced on their heads. They waved as he passed them. When he reached the old baobab, still standing proud and tall, he knew he was almost home.

Amai, Ambuya and Chikomo were already on their way to the entrance of the village as Mahachi parked the truck in the shade and climbed out. There was laughter and tears as he embraced all three of them. He savoured the moment, a moment he had been looking forward to since the day he had left. He studied each of them in turn. In their eyes he saw both delight and sadness, especially in his mother's.

They talked animatedly as they unloaded the provisions that Mahachi had brought with him for the villagers, purchased with the money from their craftwork. There were matches to light the cooking fires; green Fairy Soap for laundering; tea, powdered milk and sugar.

'You have grown much bigger since we last saw you, Mahachi, you look very fine.' Amai was smiling as she spoke, yet she wiped her hand across tearful eyes. 'Come, I will make you some breakfast, you must be hungry after your journey. Then we can sit together and you can tell us about your new life.'

'I have brought you some food from the hotel, Amai; leftovers from the kitchen.'

'I will make each of us a mug of tea to drink with your food,' said Amai.

They sat beneath a tree on the edge of the village and Mahachi spread the food on the ground beside them. There were fried potato cakes, sausages, bread and butter spread thickly with honey, and some mangoes.

'This looks very tasty, Mahachi,' said Ambuya.

As they ate, Mahachi spoke to them about his life in the town. By the time he had finished talking and answering their many questions, the sun was high in the sky.

'So you do not regret your promise to Baba?'

'No, Amai, I do not regret it. I was lonely at first but now I enjoy my life at the hotel, although there are things that I miss. Are you going fishing today, Chikomo?'

'Yes, I am. Do you want to come with me?'

'Do I want to come with you? Of course I do.'

They all laughed. 'Chikomo is joking,' said Amai touching Mahachi's arm. 'We all know that nothing could stop you.'

On the banks of the Hippo Pool, Chikomo and Mahachi took out their spears and together they walked into the shallows.

'It is so good to be back here, Chikomo. I have thought of the Hippo Pool many times and imagined you fishing here in the cool water, as I worked at my place in the hot kitchen.'

'I have missed you very much Mahachi. I had no one to talk to at night.'

'Now that I have passed my driving test I will be able to visit you regularly.'

'Do you promise?' There was a hint of desperation in Chikomo's voice that Mahachi did not understand.

'Yes, I promise.' Mahachi looked at Chikomo; he seemed tense. 'Are you still teaching the small boys to play football?' Mahachi laughed, remembering what fun it had been for the children.

'No, I do not play football now.'

Mahachi waited for him to explain but Chikomo said nothing further. Mahachi was puzzled by his brother's reticence but he was too happy to pursue the matter then.

By late afternoon they had caught plenty of fish and dark rain clouds had formed overhead. Before the two brothers reached the village with their catch, the first spots of rain began to fall. Villagers moved into their rondavels to take shelter until the storm passed.

'Ambuya, I think we should begin to prepare the bream for the evening meal.'

'Perhaps Mahachi would like to do the cooking, today,' Ambuya teased.

'No Ambuya, I am very happy to eat whatever Amai cooks. Will you walk with me to the fields so that I can see how well the crops are growing?' This was a sign they both understood; he wanted to talk to Ambuya in private.

'Ambuya, when I left the village there was sorrow at the loss of Baba. Now that I have returned, I sense a new sadness within Amai and Chikomo that I do not understand. What has happened here?'

'You see much, my grandson; things that are hidden from others. Your mother has had many difficulties but it would be unwise to discuss them here,' she said in a low voice. 'It would be better if you speak to Chikomo tonight, in the privacy of your rondavel.'

After dark the two brothers retired for the night. The village was silent and sleeping when, in a quiet voice, Chikomo told Mahachi all that had happened. 'Amai is not happy with Usai's betrothal.'

'Is she not? I myself was surprised by what Usai told me but it is not our place to question his decisions; only Baba could have done that. Usai is the head of our family now.'

'Also there was an accident at the minefield,' Chikomo continued.

'The minefield? I had not heard.'

Chikomo told Mahachi about Pita; his own torment and recovery. The two brothers talked far into the night. 'I am so pleased that you are back, Mahachi, I wish it had not been necessary for you to leave.'

That night, as they slept, Mahachi's hand rested reassuringly on Chikomo's arm.

Mahachi was reluctant to take leave of his mother the following day. 'Walk with me before I go, Amai. Tell me why Usai's betrothal does not please you as it should.'

They strolled along the dirt road. 'I was disappointed that he did not choose Chipo but it is not for me to question Usai's choice of wife.'

'I too was surprised.'

'It is a source of gossip in the village that Usai and Neli will be living in the chalet together, after the civil marriage. It causes embarrassment to our family.'

'You do not approve of the civil marriage?'

'I would have preferred the traditional marriage to be held first.'

'So, once the traditional marriage is performed the gossip will stop and you will be happy.'

'I hope so Mahachi, but I hear that other young men from our village have married maidens from urban areas. I am told their families have many difficulties.' She looked at her son. 'Have you met Neli, Mahachi?'

His mind recalled Neli's pristine appearance and Usai's words, 'she does not believe in some of the old customs.'

'No Amai, I have not met her. I have seen her working at the chemist shop but we have never spoken.'

He wanted to say something that would put his mother's mind at rest. But in his heart Mahachi did not believe that Amai's life would be easy with Neli as a member of her family.

9

Usai took one last look around his chalet before retiring for the night. Dorcas, the domestic he employed two days a week, had worked hard to make the rooms clean and tidy for tomorrow, the day of his civil marriage, when Neli would begin her life here as his wife. Usai opened his wardrobe and looked at the new white shirt, the grey trousers and the colourful tie he would be wearing to the ceremony.

'You must wear a tie,' Neli had told him.

'I have never worn one before.'

'It is expected, Usai. I will buy one for you, to match the dress I shall be wearing.'

Usai turned off the lights and climbed into bed. Lying in the darkness he imagined Neli sleeping there beside him. He hoped they would have many children. Neli would stay at home to look after them and, as their family grew, he would take some of them to live in the village, to Amai and Ambuya, who would help to raise them. How pleased Amai would be to have grandchildren sleeping in her rondavel. He smiled contentedly. He closed his eyes and fell asleep.

Neli sat on a stool in her bedroom, in the Eastern Township. *This is the last night I shall sleep in my father's house; tomorrow I begin a new life with Usai.* The thought filled her with pleasure.

She regarded her reflection in the dressing table mirror. Her hair had recently been trimmed; a neat cap of black curls framed her face. She had just finished painting her nails a deep red; a matching lipstick stood on the dressing table, ready to be applied in the morning. They had been chosen from a selection of cosmetics, sold at the chemist shop.

On a hanger in her small wardrobe was an attractive silk dress in shades of pink and lavender, made by the local dressmaker. It was simple in design, an A-line with elbow-length sleeves and a scooped neckline. The waist was slightly fitted to show the outline of her figure. A pair of black high-heeled sandals stood on the floor below the dress.

She put a small pill into her mouth and washed it down with water. In bed, she visualised the years of happiness that lay before her. She would continue to work at the chemist shop and when their children were born she would employ one of the young women from the township as a nanny, so that she herself could return to her job. The small family she was planning would have a comfortable life and be well educated. She closed her eyes and drifted into sleep.

Mahachi was standing by the open window of his hotel bedroom, gazing down at the lamplit gardens. *How beautiful they look.* The leaves were still green and lush even though the rains had ended. Frangipani flowers were releasing their powerful scent into the night air; a light evening breeze blew in through the window, brushing his cheek and making the air in the room feel cool. He watched people strolling along the garden paths, clothed in the smart outfits they wore in the evenings.

He moved away from the window and looked at the clothes that were hanging on a hook behind his bedroom door: a new blue shirt and dark blue trousers. He had bought them especially for Usai's marriage. On the table was a small box; it contained a gold ring.

In spite of the misgivings that Mahachi and his family

shared, he was determined to make tomorrow a happy, memorable day for his beloved brother.

It was late morning when Usai parked his car in the car park of the River Hotel. He walked into the hotel foyer where Mahachi was waiting for him. They grinned at each another.

'You look very smart, Mahachi.'

'So do you. I have not seen you wearing a tie before. Is it customary on these occasions?'

'According to Neli it is.'

'Should I be wearing one?'

'No, I do not think so. Anyway it is too late now. You look fine.'

'Are you ready for this, Usai?'

'I am feeling a little nervous but yes, I am ready. I was told that the man should arrive first.'

'We had better go then.'

They walked across Main Street to their destination which was a small brick building with a corrugated iron roof, painted red. The building was one storied and similar in design to the post office and the police station. Not far away, the thunderous sound of The Falls now in full flood could be heard.

'We will wait outside until Neli and Khumalo arrive,' said Usai. His eyes searched the road for a glimpse of Khumalo's blue car. 'I wonder why Neli has not arrived yet,' he said a few minutes later.

Mahachi looked at the large clock on the wall inside the building. 'Usai, your ceremony is at midday and it is still only eleven-forty. Neli will be here soon I am sure.'

'Where is the ring, Mahachi?'

'It is in here.' He patted his trouser pocket.

'Let me see it.'

Mahachi took out the box and opened the lid. The shiny unmarked ring was plain and unadorned, the kind that many women wore.

60

It was five minutes to twelve when Neli and Khumalo arrived. Khumalo was dressed in a grey suit and Neli was wearing the most beautiful dress Usai had ever seen. The vibrant pinks and lavender complimented her skin. There was a touch of red on Neli's lips and nails, and she was smiling radiantly. She rushed towards him and he clasped her hands in his.

The four of them walked inside the building; the Registry Office was to the right. The walls were painted cream and the concrete floor had been polished to give it a more attractive appearance, but there was nothing in the vicinity to suggest impending matrimonial joy.

A man came through a nearby door and looked in their direction. 'Usai and Nelisiwe, please come this way.'

They entered a small room. Sunlight streamed in through the window, making the surroundings attractive and cheerful. Music was playing quietly in the background. Greenery trailed down the sides of a pedestal on which a large colourful flower arrangement stood; the intense fragrance of the lilies perfumed the air. A man was standing behind a teak table, set on a rich red carpet.

He smiled warmly at them. 'Good afternoon,' he said. 'Please come forward.'

The ceremony began.

The four of them stepped outside, smiling happily. Usai carried a marriage certificate in his hand.

'So now you are married; *makorokoto* my brother, congratulations.' Mahachi shook Usai's hand. '*Makorokoto* Neli,' Mahachi said, shaking her hand too. He noticed that her other hand rested on the crook of her arm, a traditional gesture of respect for the brother of her husband. To Mahachi it was an encouraging sign.

'Thank you,' she said.

'I have a surprise for you, Usai,' said Mahachi. 'We are

going to have a celebration lunch at the River Hotel. I arranged it with the manager, Mr Jackson.'

They had been allocated a table in the corner of the dining room, overlooking the gardens. In the centre of the table was a small floral decoration of bright orange marigolds and colourful gazanias.

When they were seated, the waiter brought each of them a cool fruit drink. The rims of the tall glasses were frosted with sugar and decorated with slices of orange and lemon. As they slowly sipped their drinks Usai, Neli and Khumalo gazed about them, fascinated by their surroundings. They had not eaten at an international hotel before.

'If you are ready, we can help ourselves to some food,' said Mahachi.

He led the way to the buffet and walked the length of it with them. 'This table is the cold buffet, with different kinds of salami and sliced meat as well as a variety of salads.' He moved on to the next table. 'Here is the hot food,' he said, lifting the lids of the containers to reveal their contents. 'There is *sadza*, potatoes or rice, beef or chicken casserole, and plenty of cooked vegetables to choose from. Over there is the dessert table,' he said, pointing. 'Those are the sweet foods, the puddings.'

Usai, Neli and Khumalo looked bewildered by the choices available to them; especially the large colourful selection of raw salad vegetables and the creamy confections which they were not accustomed to eating.

'Mahachi, I would prefer the hot food. It would be best if I follow your example and choose what you choose,' commented Usai. Khumalo and Neli agreed. Mahachi took a warm plate and using the serving spoons he selected food from dishes which he thought they would enjoy.

At their table the atmosphere was relaxed and happy; they talked and laughed as they savoured the food.

'I thought the man who conducted the ceremony was very

pleasant. I felt nervous at first but he made me feel comfortable,' said Usai.

'I liked the room and the flowers,' said Neli. 'It looked very attractive. But most of all I like my ring.' Smiling, she raised her hand to admire the unblemished gold.

'I was expecting a longer ceremony,' Mahachi commented.

'I did not know what to expect,' said Usai.

'A short ceremony is usual at a Registry Office, I believe,' said Khumalo. 'I was married at my village in the south. The marriage and celebrations lasted four days.' He chuckled.

'This chicken is very tasty with the sweet potatoes and pumpkin, Mahachi.' said Neli.

'Yes it is.' Turning to Neli, Usai said, 'Perhaps Mahachi could discover how it is made and you can cook it for us.'

When they had finished eating, the waiter came to remove their empty plates. He returned shortly, wheeling a trolley. When he reached their table he said, 'Compliments of the chef.'

On the beautifully appointed trolley was a cake covered in smooth white icing. Round the bottom were tiny shell shapes; on the top, the names of Usai and Neli were decoratively entwined, with skilful piping. Mahachi was surprised; the cake had not been ordered. A small card at the side of the cake explained. Usai picked it up and read it aloud.

> To Usai, Baba's first-born son,
> Congratulations and best wishes,
> From Mpofu and the kitchen staff.

Usai choked back tears as he read the words. He turned his face away for a moment, to regain his composure. The waiter cut them each a slice of the iced sponge cake and put it on a small plate with a cake fork. Mahachi picked up the fork and the others copied what he did.

'Mmm, this is delicious,' said Usai, now fully composed. 'I think I will take another slice.'

'Me too,' said Mahachi, who had recently developed a sweet tooth. 'The remains will be put into a box and given to you to take home, Usai.'

Outside in the car park they took leave of each other. Khumalo said goodbye to his daughter. They would meet from time to time but she was no longer his. 'You have been a generous daughter, Neli; make Usai a good wife.' He shook hands with Usai. 'I look forward to the traditional marriage and to seeing Little Father again.' He turned to Mahachi and thanked him for the meal. 'I have other daughters who are not yet married. I am sure one of them would make you a fine wife, Mahachi,' he chuckled.

Usai embraced his brother. 'Thank you for being my witness and for the celebration meal.' He had been deeply touched by the gesture. 'What a very fine brother I have.'

'And so have I. When I first came to the town, lonely and afraid, it was a comfort to me to know that you were nearby. Today was to thank you for that … and also for the driving lessons.'

10

Inside the chalet, Usai and Neli gazed at each other. No more self-imposed repression, no further sexual restraint between them, no nightly fantasising. He pressed his lips to her soft velvety cheek, breathing in the smell of her lightly perfumed skin.

In the bedroom, both unclothed, Usai explored the outline of Neli's figure, the curve of her waist, the sensuous rounded hips. She moaned softly. He held her close, feeling her voluptuous body against his. Usai led her to the bed, all his self-control gone.

As the sun edged its way above the horizon, the sleeping lovers lay on their backs, hot and uncovered, their skin glowing with perspiration. The heat of the day began to enter through the open window. It was Neli who stirred first. She turned her head and looked sleepily at Usai; his eyes were closed, his breathing soft and even.

Slipping quietly off the bed Neli went to the bathroom and ran a bath. Stepping into the warm water she slid beneath it to soak. Closing her eyes she revisited her journey through the pleasures of the night into full womanhood.

Usai surfaced from sleep and reached out to touch Neli. He found the place beside him empty. Opening his eyes he saw her through the open bathroom door, her head resting on the edge of the bathtub. Joining her he stepped into the opposite end of the bath. They soaked for a while without speaking, their legs entwined. Usai felt the touch of Neli's soft silken thighs against his. Gently he encircled one of her nipples with his fingertip and felt the nipple harden. Neli murmured as she felt the erotic sensation reach the deep, secret places of her body.

In the first weeks of their life together Usai and Neli spent most of their free time at home, making love or talking. Sometimes they strolled along the river path, once in a while they joined old friends at the coffee bar to exchange news, but mostly they preferred the pleasure of their own company. They settled into a routine.

'I have asked Dorcas to come in three days a week, to do the cleaning and laundry,' said Usai one evening as he stood in the kitchen, watching Neli prepare the relish for their evening meal. 'Also she can help me unload the boot of the car when I bring home the shopping.'

At the end of the day, after they had eaten, they would sometimes sit quietly together on the sitting-room sofa and read. Usai preferred the books he borrowed from the National Parks Office; pictorial books, with brilliant illustrations of local wildlife or indigenous plants. Neli borrowed love stories from the small local library and enjoyed reading magazines. Difficult to acquire, they were donated to her by customers.

Usai opened the bathroom cabinet one day to find the shelves full of small bottles, packets and boxes from the chemist shop. 'What are all these?'

Neli picked up one of the packets. 'These pills are painkillers. And that,' she said pointing to a bottle, 'is antiseptic for bathing wounds.'

'Are you planning to transfer the whole chemist shop to our bathroom?' he asked, amused. 'Why have you bought them?'

'In case we are unwell and need a cure.'

'You know that I visit the *nganga* if I need *muti*.'

66

'Now you will have no need of his medicines.' She smiled brightly.

'I will always use the *nganga*, unless he is unable to cure me.' He took a small box containing soap from the cabinet and held it to his nose, inhaling the delicate floral fragrance. 'I hope you are not expecting me to use this soap. What would my tourists think, if I greeted them smelling like a jasmine bush?'

'No, the soap is mine; it makes me alluring. That is what it says on the box. Look,' she said, showing him the label.

Usai laughed. 'Neli you are already alluring, you have no need of such soap.'

'But I like the smell of the perfume on my skin.'

He smiled at her indulgently.

Neli chose not to tell Usai that she was taking the pill. She did not wish to spoil their happiness and she knew, from one of their conversations, that he would not approve. One evening she had mentioned the Family Planning Clinic in the township.

'I have heard of the clinic,' he had said, 'but I want as many children as possible.'

'But Usai, a large family has many mouths to feed; small families have more money.'

'How big is a small family?'

'It is usually two children.'

'Only two! If I fathered so few children my family and friends would say, "Usai, is that all your manhood can produce?" How humiliated I would be. I hope for sons who will share my interest in the Zambezi Valley, and daughters who will bring me a fine *lobola*, to add to the family herd. I do not intend to use the Family Planning Clinic and I do not want you to visit it either.'

Neli decided to keep her own council.

* * *

'I have a free day today. I would like us to take a drive south of the Zambezi Valley, to do some game viewing,' said Usai, one Sunday morning. 'You might enjoy it.'

'Perhaps,' said Neli. She had previously declared her lack of interest in the local flora and fauna.

They sped south, away from the river. The air was warm and they opened the car windows to create a breeze. The narrow dirt road they were following had an uneven surface. The vehicle jerked and jolted its way along; Neli bounced up and down.

'This is very uncomfortable,' she said.

'The conditions will improve soon.'

Suddenly the road widened and the soil became sandy; as it passed beneath the wheels, it felt soft and smooth.

'That feels much better.'

'You should close your window, Neli,' said Usai, as he hastily wound up his own. A cloud of sand was beginning to drift inside the car.

Further on, Usai slowed the vehicle and stopped. Standing immobile beneath some trees was a small herd of antelope with two calves. Usai and Neli sat quietly watching them.

'What are they called?' asked Neli.

'They are sable antelope; these are females.'

'All of them? How can you be sure?'

'Because they are dark brown. Can you see the male over there?' he asked, pointing into the bush.

'Yes I can see him; he is black.'

'These are my favourite antelope.'

'Why do you like them so much?'

'They are proud and strong, and they have such magnificent curved horns. Do you not like them?'

'Yes, I like the animals but I am not enjoying the journey; I have been thrown from side to side, shaken about and now I am covered in sand,' she exaggerated.

Usai laughed. 'I am used to the discomfort, it no longer troubles me. I will drive slowly from now on.'

He switched on the engine and drove on. Overhead, scavengers of the air soared and glided, in search of carrion. 'Have you noticed the vultures? They are so graceful in flight, quite different from their clumsy movements on the ground.'

'They are such ugly birds.'

'Yes they are but we need them to pick the bones clean, and leave the bush hygienic.'

Stopping the car to scan the area with his binoculars, Usai noticed a movement in the distance. 'Look over there under the trees, in the long grass; *shumba.*' He handed Neli the binoculars.

'I can see them: a male, two females and four cubs.'

'What are they doing?'

'The male lion is lying on his back with his legs in the air … two of the cubs are climbing over his great body. They are so tiny. Oh look, one of them is nibbling his left ear … and there is a fourth biting his tail, tugging it backwards and forwards.' She laughed excitedly. 'They are like small children, playing with their father. He is being very patient with them.'

Usai was glad to see her enthusiasm. 'The two females have started to move forward; they are staring into the distance, probably on the lookout for herds and their next meal.' Usai turned on the ignition. 'I am feeling hungry myself. I think it is time for us to drive back.'

'Next time I come I will wear different clothes, a dress is unsuitable; and I will cover my head with a scarf to keep out the sand.'

He looked at her, surprised. *Next time I come.* The remark pleased him.

11

During his free time in the afternoons, Mahachi often took a walk, to find a shady place and cool down after the lunch period, the hottest part of the day in the kitchen.

Wearing cotton trousers, a T-shirt and flip-flops, he walked towards the foyer on his way out of the hotel, unaware of the admiring glances he was receiving from some of the women in the lounge. He was now taller than most of the staff; his appearance was no longer immature. He was a tall, handsome young man.

The front entrance of the hotel was crowded with tourists chattering excitedly. They were white-water rafters, making their way to the minibuses parked in the drive. The vehicles would take them and their equipment, to a place above the embarkation point, in the bowels of the gorge near the Boiling Pot.

Mahachi paused by the door to let the tourists pass. One young woman who walked past him had bright blue eyes and her hair was braided into a long plait. She reminded him of his recent encounter at The Falls. As he regarded her he smiled, recollecting the sensation of soft hair trailing along his arm; she returned his smile, misunderstanding. Mahachi watched her board one of the minibuses and take a seat by a window overlooking the hotel entrance. When the heavily laden minibus moved slowly out of the drive, he noticed that she turned her head to look at him.

Once outside the hotel, Mahachi walked to The Falls and

stood for a while at one of the viewing points enjoying the feel of spray on his face, cool and refreshing. Strolling through the rainforest and out into the bright sunlight he sat down on some large boulders and peered down to the bottom of the gorge.

On the opposite side he could see a small stony beach by the swirling waters of the Boiling Pot. People in lifejackets were stepping into large yellow rafts. He recognised one of them; the young woman with the long plait who had passed him at the hotel. He saw her climb over the side of one of the rafts and sit down at the front, taking hold of the ropes that hung there.

Mahachi watched as the rafts were pushed off the beach and into the water; the oarsmen battling to row into centre stream. The swift-flowing current carried the rafts towards a bend in the gorge, and suddenly they were out of sight. Mahachi stood up. In the distance, downstream, he could see a place of great beauty, with thickly forested islands and high banks, past which the rafts would soon float on their way to the white waters of the rapids beyond.

The following afternoon, Mahachi decided to take the river path and walk from the Devil's Cataract upstream. As he began his stroll a young woman joined him. She was wearing a sleeveless T-shirt, cropped trousers and flat sandals. A long plait hung over one shoulder; a bag swung from the other.

'Didn't I see you in the foyer yesterday, after lunch?' she asked.

Mahachi turned and looked at her, he recognised her immediately. 'Yes you did, you were with a group of white-water rafters.'

'Yes that's right. May I walk with you? I'd like to see the upper river. I'm Janacen, by the way.'

'I am pleased to meet you. My name is Mahachi.'

They set off at a gentle pace, pausing for a while to watch some malachite kingfishers flitting from branch to branch above the water's edge; their turquoise plumage shimmering in the sunlight. A sudden screech came from above. A fish eagle was slowly circling overhead; its enormous black wings tilted and turned as it cruised the river in search of food.

'What beautiful birds you have in this part of the world. We saw many yesterday from the rafts.'

'Is there white-water rafting in your country?'

'Yes in the spring, when the snow on the mountains melts and the rivers rush down to the sea.'

Mahachi had no idea what she meant. 'I would like to hear about your land. Shall we sit here in the shade for a while?' he ventured, pointing to a seat.

'If you like.'

They sat facing the opposite shore, gazing at the moving water, and Janacen told him something of her world in the far north. How cold it was in winter, when silent flakes of snow fell from the sky, covering the land in a white blanket. She talked of the long hours of winter darkness, when the sun hardly appeared; her words painted him a picture of frozen rivers and mountain peaks. Then, smiling, she spoke of the thaw when the snow melted and the country was green once more; of the long hours of daylight when the sun barely set. Mahachi tried to visualise this cold northern land.

That night Mahachi dreamt he was walking through the rainforest and the ground was covered in cold white snow, which sparkled in the sunlight. His feet made deep imprints in it. When he looked at The Falls they had frozen into a solid wall of spiky fingers which hung over the edge of the precipice and stretched down into the gorge below. When he awoke, Mahachi was relieved to feel that the warmth from the rising sun had entered his bedroom.

The following day Mahachi's and Janacen's paths crossed again, by chance or design. When they reached the seat on the river path, Janacen said, 'Today it's your turn to tell me about your life here by the Zambezi.'

They sat closer together this time. Mahachi told Janacen how he had wanted to be a fisherman; he talked about his village and family, and why he became a chef at the hotel. Sitting so close, he noticed that she had a pleasant scent about her and that her fair skin was turning a golden colour. He felt at ease in her company, as though he had known her for much longer than two days.

'Are you married, Mahachi, or planning to marry?'

'No, not yet.'

'Me neither. Will you marry someone from your village?'

'Usually our maidens marry young men from other villages or towns, and we choose wives who are not from our community.'

'Why is that?'

'My father once told me that marriage to people from the same village can lead to unhealthy children.'

'Oh.' They sat quietly watching the river. 'Do you live in a house Mahachi, in one of the suburbs, beyond the hotel?'

'No, I am resident at the hotel. I am lucky. I was given room number fifteen, which overlooks the swimming pool and the gardens.'

Walking back to the hotel, she linked her arm through his in a friendly manner. Mahachi stopped. 'Is it customary in your country for young people to touch in this way? Would your father not be angry?' he asked.

'No. As adults we can do as we please; touch, hold hands, sleep together.'

'Is it not necessary for you to be married first?'

'No, why do you ask? Am I doing something inappropriate?'

'It is not our custom to touch before marriage, Janacen. It is taboo. Also I could be dismissed from the hotel, if I was seen behaving this way with a guest.'

'Oh, I see. I'm sorry.' Janacen withdrew her arm and blushed, embarrassed. For a while they walked without speaking.

'I noticed that your cheeks became pink when you pulled your arm away from mine. It made you look very pretty. I liked the feel of your arm holding mine, Janacen. I hope we meet again,' he said softly.

At the end of the day Mahachi stood for a long time in the shower, letting the tepid water pour over his head and body, cleansing and cooling. Afterwards he wrapped a bath towel round his waist, hardly bothering to dry himself. There was a knock at the bedroom door.

'Come in,' he said, assuming it was Mpofu or one of the other kitchen staff. Janacen stepped into the room, dressed in a colourful kaftan; her hair, no longer plaited, hung loosely down her back.

'Janacen! What are you doing here?' he asked, surprised. He peered outside to see if there was anyone in the passageway, before closing the door quickly.

'I would like to spend some time with you, where we can't be seen if we break your taboos. I thought you would be glad to see me but if you want me to leave, I will.'

Mahachi stared at her; his expression slowly softened. 'You should not be here,' he said, without conviction.

She moved close to him. 'I know.' Her head tilted to one side, as she gazed at him with her twinkling blue eyes.

He touched her hair tentatively at first, surprised by its softness; he ran his hands through it, feeling its unfamiliar texture between his fingers. 'Let me see what you look like,' he said in a quiet voice, touching her kaftan.

She pulled it over her head; she was naked. Mahachi's eyes feasted on her body. It was the colour of cream except where the sun had touched her skin and turned it golden brown. The pale pink nipples were so different from the rich brown ones he had seen, being teased into the mouths of hungry

74

infants. The hair on her body was as pale as the mane that flowed down to her waist.

His hands caressed her shoulders and arms. She loosened the towel round his waist and let it drop to the floor; her fingers moved down his spine making gooseflesh on his back. Mahachi clasped her in his arms, feeling the naked body of a woman against his for the first time. Inhaling the enticing smell of her femininity, he drew her to the bed, unable to contain his longing for her. Once inside her his body erupted into a spasm of exquisite pleasure.

They lay side by side. 'Janacen I …' She pressed her fingers to his lips, silencing him. Taking his hand, she guided it over her body, showing him where to touch her, how to give her the most pleasure. He listened to the sounds she made, the soft moans and gentle murmurs; watched her face as it changed with each new sensation. They fondled gently at first, then with mounting urgency.

With a hand resting on the other's body, they slept facing each other. When dawn came and Mahachi opened his eyes, he was alone.

He showered quickly and went down to the kitchen. As he worked his mind would not rest; fragments of the night returned unbidden.

'Are you unwell, Mahachi?' Mpofu enquired. 'I have asked you a question three times now and you have not replied.'

'I am sorry, Mpofu, I have something on my mind.'

'You must concentrate on your work; daydreaming is for your free time.'

After lunch, Mahachi did not go for his usual walk, he went to his room. He wanted to be alone, to think. No sounds came from outside; people would return to the pool area later, when it was cooler. In the quiet of his room he lay on his bed contemplating. Everything he had done the previous night was contrary to his traditional beliefs. *I should have sent her away*, he scolded himself. *I hope she leaves the hotel and we never meet again.*

But his feelings were ambivalent. He closed his eyes and let his mind travel back, recalling every moment they had spent together. The words they had spoken to each other, the feelings they had shared. He longed to see her soon, wanted her to visit him in his room again.

As he worked in the kitchen later that afternoon, preparing the evening meal, Mahachi glanced out of the window more often than usual, hoping to catch a glimpse of Janacen. When his work for the day was complete he climbed the stairs and walked along the corridor to his room, to wait. He listened to every footstep in the passageway outside, anticipating a knock on his door, but it did not come. In bed he dozed; it was past midnight when he finally fell asleep.

The sensation of a warm body pressed against his brought him back to consciousness; he felt an arm across his chest, a cheek pressed to his shoulder. He turned over and held her close. His hands needed no prompting; her cries of pleasure came in waves.

Hot and exhausted, they lay stroking each other tenderly as they talked in low voices.

'I stayed awake for a long time hoping you would come.'

'Our group was taken to see the Shangaan Dancers. I came as soon as the dancing finished.'

'So you are interested in traditional dancing?'

'Yes. I enjoyed it when the narrator told us about the spirit world, and the dancers performed a dance to drive away evil spirits, although I did not understand everything.'

'Did you not? Only evil people become evil spirits. Our people believe that when we die our spirit inhabits the body of an animal or bird. In my village it is the Heughlin's robin which is our totem.'

She turned over on to her back and lay without speaking

76

for a while. 'So one day you will be a beautiful bird.' She turned her head and smiled at him.

'Did you like other dances?'

'Yes I liked the fertility dance.'

His hand stroked her belly. 'I would have demonstrated it for you here, you could have joined in,' he laughed. 'I will show you tomorrow.'

She looked at him, her expression sad. Mahachi stopped laughing. 'What is it?'

'We leave tomorrow.'

'Leave? Where are you going?'

'We are flying to Kariba.'

'Can you not stay here for longer?'

'I can't.'

She saw the disappointment on his face and felt her own unwillingness to depart. Together they watched as the dawn sky changed colour. The melancholy song of the boubou bird floated in through the open window.

'Do not go.'

'I must.'

Yet they held one another tightly, reluctant to separate. Finally Janacen took his hands in hers and kissed them. She put on her dress, slipped quietly out of the door and was gone.

Mahachi said very little that day. The heaviness in the pit of his stomach was at times so great that he had difficulty breathing. That night as he lay in bed, surrounded by her lingering scent, his yearning for her was overwhelming. She had stolen his peace of mind.

It was mid-afternoon. Mahachi and Mpofu were sitting next to each other at the staff dining table, eating their lunch. Mahachi picked at his food, he had no appetite. He sat in silence, alone with his thoughts.

'Are you going for a walk after lunch today, Mahachi?' asked Mpofu.

'Probably, why do you ask?'

'I would like to come with you.'

They walked towards the statue of David Livingstone. 'Let us sit down for a while. I want to talk to you, Mahachi,' Mpofu said. They found a seat in the shade.

'Why do you want to talk to me?'

'I know about the young woman who visited your room.'

'You know … How do you know?'

'People in the laundry room gossip when they are washing the bed linen. Also you have become very quiet recently; some of the staff noticed that you look unhappy.'

'Is everybody discussing me? Am I going to be reported to Mr Jackson? I might lose my job and will no longer be able to support my family,' said Mahachi, distraught.

'No. No. Nobody is going to report you. The staff would never do such a thing but we are concerned about you.'

Mahachi sighed. 'I cannot stop thinking about her, Mpofu; the things we did together.'

Mpofu's voice was sympathetic. 'Such women are not for us, Mahachi. They come for a short visit and are soon gone. The unhappiness you are suffering will pass. You should talk to Usai.' They sat for a while without speaking. 'There is something else.' Mpofu handed Mahachi a small cardboard packet. 'Look inside.' Mahachi opened the packet and took out one of the foil sachets he found there. 'Have you seen one of these before, Mahachi?'

'No, what is this?'

'It is a condom.' Mpofu opened the sealed foil sachet and showed Mahachi what was inside. 'Men wear them when they go with women.'

'Why would they do that?'

'It is a contraceptive. Some people use them to prevent pregnancy but they are also used to protect you against diseases; the diseases that can pass between a man and a woman.'

An image of Baba flashed across Mahachi's mind; he felt a wave of panic. 'Do you think I have caught a disease, Mpofu?'

'No I do not believe so, but you might have done. I think it would be wise to make an appointment to see Dr Meyer, to be sure.'

Mahachi lay awake that night for a long time, considering Mpofu's words of advice. *How little I know*, he thought. Yet his experience with Janacen had been so tender, he found it hard to believe that anything unpleasant would come of it. Nevertheless, the next morning he made an appointment with Dr Meyer, the general practitioner.

It was three weeks later that an envelope marked 'Confidential' arrived for Mahachi, at reception. The result of his first blood test was negative.

12

Usai studied Mahachi as he crossed the road and came in through the door of the coffee bar. He seemed different. He walked with more confidence and self-assurance than previously and there was something else, an elusive quality that Usai could not fathom. He noticed that Mahachi's eyes lingered on some of the young women he passed. Usai smiled to himself.

Mahachi was responding to a note handed to him by Everjoy. It was a request from Usai to meet him here. Mahachi shook his brother's hand and sat down opposite him. 'I am very glad to see you, Usai.'

'And I you, my brother.'

'How is Neli?'

'She is fine.' Usai smiled at the thought of her.

'You are looking very relaxed and happy. Neli must be looking after you well.'

Usai laughed. 'Yes she is. It will soon be time for you to start looking for a wife.'

Mahachi ignored the comment. He intended to talk to Usai, to tell him about Janacen, but he needed privacy, a time when they could be alone together.

Changing the subject he asked, 'Why did you want to see me, Usai?'

'Well first of all, we have not met since the civil ceremony and I was keen to see you.' He paused for a moment. 'Also I have a favour to ask. I want to take some provisions to the village but my car is too small. I need the use of Baba's old truck and your help.'

'Of course I will help you. Actually I am free on Monday and Tuesday of next week. I intend to go to the village anyway; you could come with me.'

'Yes, I could do that. I will take two days leave. Let us meet at six-thirty on Monday morning in the hotel car park.'

Just after dawn on Monday, Usai parked his car at the River Hotel and joined Mahachi who was waiting for him in Baba's old truck. They set off along Main Street.

'Where are the provisions? Mahachi asked.

'We have to collect them from a farm that breeds livestock. It is to the south, just outside of town.'

'You are collecting livestock?'

'Yes, I am going to buy some goats and poultry, in readiness for my marriage feast.'

'But we have plenty of goats in the family herd.'

'Yes I know but I do not want to use them. One day Chikomo will want to marry; he will need some of the family goats for his *lobola*.'

'What about the chickens?'

'Some are for the feast; Ambuya can raise the rest of them for eggs and meat. Neli and I enjoyed the chicken dishes we ate at the hotel. We are hoping that you will cook one of them for us.'

'I will be glad to. I must speak to the poultry chef and ask him how they are prepared and cooked, then I can choose one that people in the village will enjoy.'

They had reached the outskirts of town and were travelling along a wide, tree-lined road. The undulating tarmac stretched for miles into the distance; there was not a vehicle in sight. On the opposite side of the road a signpost indicated Victoria Falls Airport. *Janacen flew from there to Kariba*, Mahachi thought. He glanced along the lane to the airstrip as he drove past it, half expecting to see her standing there.

81

Mahachi was no longer consumed by thoughts of Janacen but his memories of her had not diminished. He remembered every detail of her face, the sound of her voice and the experiences they had shared; experiences that aroused in him a curiosity about other women. He found himself staring at them, his eyes looking directly into theirs, wondering.

'Turn left here,' said Usai. 'The farm is about two miles further on.'

Mahachi drove along a dirt road and into the farmyard where he parked the truck.

'I will go and look for the farmer,' Usai said, as he climbed out of the vehicle. He had visited the farm recently and already agreed on a price for two large goats, six speckled hens and a cockerel.

While he was waiting, Mahachi wandered towards one of the pens. He stood looking down at the pink-skinned pigs, quite different from the wild grey bush pigs and the coarse-haired warthogs that he was familiar with.

'Will you open the back of the truck, Mahachi? I want to put the goats in first,' called Usai. With the help of two farm workers, Usai led the two goats to the truck and lifted them into the back. Mahachi shut the doors quickly so they could not escape. 'I am going to fetch the chickens now,' said Usai.

Alone in the enclosure, Usai had some difficulty with the fowls. Just when he thought he had caught one, it squawked loudly and flew out of his hands. Mahachi watched in amusement as his brother rushed this way and that in an effort to grasp one of the hens. Eventually he succeeded. Clutching it firmly under one arm, he opened the gate and hurried towards the truck. When he reached it, Mahachi swiftly opened the right-hand door just far enough for the hen to be put inside.

Several of the farm workers had noticed that Usai was having difficulties and had gathered to watch. One or two of them were laughing.

'Will you help me?' Usai called out to them.

'Let me show you how it is done,' volunteered one of them. Forcing the chickens into a corner, the farm worker was able to grasp them easily. Within a short time six plump hens and a cockerel were safely inside the back of the vehicle.

Baba's old truck was perfect for transporting animals. Although it was usually without a roof and had a tailgate, it came with a detachable canopy, which had grilles along the sides, and two doors at the back. The grilles allowed air to blow through the truck, keeping it cool for the animals, but also allowing their noises to be heard.

'So, now you are expecting me to drive back through the town and on to the village with this farmyard clucking and baaing in the back of my truck. I am a respected employee of the tourist industry,' Mahachi joked, loftily. 'You drive, Usai and I will sit in the passenger seat wearing Baba's old sunglasses and hat; hopefully nobody will recognise me.'

But Baba's old truck was well known in the town and as it passed along Main Street people waved and hooted their horns. The animals could be seen and heard. Every bump in the road produced baas and squawks, as the animals were jerked against the sides of the vehicle. Mahachi slid lower down in his seat; the only part of him now visible through the front windscreen was Baba's old hat.

Usai turned left at the end of Main Street on to Zambezi Drive. When they were beyond the perimeter of the town and driving through open bush towards the village, Mahachi sat up and removed his disguise.

'I have never felt so humiliated, Usai. The kitchen staff will have plenty to say later, if any of them noticed me.' Mahachi sniggered and finally they both burst out laughing.

It was a long time since Mahachi had laughed.

Chikomo launched himself at his brothers, laughing with happiness. 'Let me show you what I am doing,' he said excitedly, taking each of them by the hand and pulling them in the direction of the new rondavel.

Amai laughed. 'Chikomo, give your brothers some time to rest after their journey.' She embraced Usai and Mahachi. 'It is good to see you both.'

Mahachi opened the back of the truck; the sound of animals could be heard.

'What have you brought us?' Amai asked.

'Two goats for the marriage feast and some chickens,' said Usai.

Amai looked inside the truck. 'They are fine healthy animals. We will put the goats with the family herd. Why have you brought us chickens?'

'Some are for the marriage feast; Mahachi is going to cook us one of the chicken dishes they serve at the hotel. I thought Ambuya could raise the rest, so that you will have eggs and meat.'

'I raised some chickens once before,' said Ambuya, who had joined them. 'I shall enjoy raising these. Perhaps Chikomo would like to build me a coop now that he has some carpentry skills. The chickens will need somewhere to roost safely at night.'

Mahachi and Usai looked at Chikomo.

'What carpentry skills are these?' asked Usai.

'That is what I was trying to show you. I am helping to build a new rondavel. Come and see.'

'You had better go and look,' said Amai. 'He will not rest until he has shown you his workmanship.'

The circle of thick poles and slim saplings which formed the outline of the wall was now covered by a pointed roof. Large poles had been skilfully shaped to form an apex.

'I have been using strips of bark to bind the poles and saplings together, round this part of the wall,' said Chikomo, pointing to the section in front of them. 'The plastering will begin soon but it will be some time before we can put the

84

thatching on the roof; the grass in the bush is not yet dry enough to harvest.'

Mahachi and Usai inspected the wall.

'Your skills are very good, Chikomo.'

'Yes indeed, you have done well. How often do you work here with the men?'

'I do this work in my spare time Mahachi, when I am not fishing. I no longer play football or games with the children.'

'I am very proud of you, little brother,' said Usai.

'So am I,' said Mahachi.

Chikomo beamed, delighted that his brothers thought well of him.

A group of maidens was standing nearby. One of them had been staring at Chikomo for some time. When he turned round, she smiled brightly at him.

He returned her smile. 'Hello Tabeth,' he said, 'how are you?'

'I am fine, thank you Chikomo.'

'I see that Amai has made us some tea,' said Mahachi. 'Shall we go?'

'I think I will stay here for a while,' Chikomo told his brothers.

Usai and Mahachi looked at each other and grinned.

'I have brought some leftovers from the hotel, including the fish cakes that you enjoy, Chikomo. If you do not come soon, there will be no food left for you,' Mahachi joked.

'I will not be long,' called Chikomo, as his brothers walked away.

'I would like to go to the Hippo Pool after we have eaten, Usai. Will you come with me?' asked Mahachi.

'Yes I had planned to go there myself. We will go together.'

Mahachi and Usai sat on the ground beneath the trees, facing the long island; the tall grass there was turning yellow. Vegetable ivory hung in large clusters from the palms.

Floating on the water of the pool were some Nile cabbages; occasionally a giant head would rise from the depths wearing one of the cabbages between its ears, like an Easter bonnet. Further upstream a flock of small yellow birds were twittering loudly as they flitted from tree to tree, collecting material to build their round nests. Hanging from the ends of branches, the nests were suspended over the water.

'I had forgotten how peaceful it is here,' said Usai, 'except for those weavers!'

'I have something to tell you; things I need to talk about, Usai.' Mahachi had finally summoned the courage to speak.

Usai tensed and looked at him sharply. He had heard words similar to those before, from Baba. They were words which had heralded the grim reaper.

'What is it?'

In a quiet voice Mahachi told him about Janacen and what had happened between them. He related his conversation with Mpofu and described the visit to Dr Meyer. When Mahachi had finished speaking, Usai sat in silence, deeply shocked.

Finally he spoke. 'I noticed a change in you when we met at the coffee bar, now I understand. I have neglected you Mahachi. I have been busy with my own life and not made contact with you as I should. I ought to have spoken to you about these things when you first moved to town. Those of us who work with tourists are vulnerable. Such a thing might have happened to me. You must be lonely in your bed, now that Janacen has gone.'

'Sometimes when I wake at night, I miss her warm body close to mine.'

'I have noticed the way you look at young women; you must be tempted. I think it is time you considered marriage. We could ask Little Father and Ambuya to help; there are many maidens in the neighbouring villages.'

'Usai, I cannot marry just anyone, not now. Modest,

bashful maidens are not for me. I need someone bold and lusty.'

'Maybe Khumalo could help. He has unmarried daughters like Neli who are much less shy.'

'I want to choose my own wife, Usai, as you did. I will not marry someone chosen by others. But I will do as you suggest and give marriage some thought.'

'You are right. It is not for me to decide who you will marry. I love you my brother.' Usai put an arm affectionately round Mahachi's shoulders. 'I want no harm to come to you; I need you to be safe and happy. We have had problems enough with Baba and Chikomo. I will meet you as often as I can in town so that we can talk as we used to.'

The meal that evening in the village was a happy family gathering, including Little Father who usually preferred to eat alone. There was a great deal of talk and laughter.

'I see that Tabeth is still showing an interest in you, Chikomo,' said Little Father. 'Now she is with other maidens when she watches you work on the rondavel,' he chuckled.

'You too have an admirer, Mahachi,' announced Ambuya.

Both Mahachi and Usai looked at their grandmother in alarm. *Surely she does not know about Janacen*, thought Mahachi.

'The young woman lives at the other end of the village,' Ambuya continued. 'She has spent much time looking in your direction since you arrived. She is not to everyone's taste; less modest than other maidens, a little bolder perhaps than some prefer but still a fine maiden.'

Mahachi made no comment but he sat scrutinising his grandmother. How curious that she should choose those words, so similar to the ones he had spoken to Usai earlier.

It was long after dark when the family went to their rondavels to sleep. Usai, Mahachi and Chikomo were sleeping in the same rondavel they had used in childhood.

'Well, little brother, what is all this talk about Tabeth?' asked Usai.

'I am in love,' announced Chikomo, grandly. Usai and Mahachi tried to stifle their laughter.

'Why are you laughing at me? Have you not noticed that since your last visit I have started to become a man?'

Mahachi and Usai pulled Chikomo playfully down on to the floor between them. Mahachi ran his finger along Chikomo's upper lip. 'Yes I can see how manly you have become. What is this thick bushy growth I feel,' he said, as he touched the barely visible hair. 'Where will we find a razor large and sharp enough to shave it off?'

Usai was examining Chikomo's lower legs. 'And the hairs on your legs are becoming so long, that they will soon cover your feet and you will trip over them as you walk down to the Hippo Pool.'

Chikomo was lying on his back laughing delightedly. He rarely received so much attention; his nights were lonely in the rondavel. How glad he was to have his brothers with him once more. He slept between them, his body touching each of theirs.

The following morning, after a breakfast of *rapoko* porridge, Usai went to talk to Little Father about the traditional marriage ceremony, while Amai and Mahachi packed the truck with craftwork to be delivered to the Craft Village.

'Mahachi, I have prepared a list of purchases I want you to make, to bring with you to Usai's marriage celebrations after the harvest,' Amai said. She handed him a scrap of paper on which she had written down a number of items. 'I am looking forward to meeting Neli. Do you like her?'

'She was pleasant and respectful when we met at the civil ceremony and also she is making Usai happy. I like her for that, Amai.'

The temperature had dropped to twenty-five degrees Celsius; it was now the middle of the cool, dry season. The rains had been good this year, the crops plentiful. In the fields, women were reaping the dried millet and maize; in the village, storage huts were being repaired and secured, for the bounty that would soon fill them.

Amai, together with other village women, had been working for many days, cutting down the grass-like millet and the tall tasselled maize, carrying the dehydrated plants to the side of the fields, where they were laid out on the ground.

Ambuya sat on a blanket outside her rondavel, watching as she crocheted a tablecloth for the Craft Village. Near her several small children were playing; their laughter could be heard by their mothers in the fields. A toddler wearing a bright yellow dress waddled unsteadily across the blanket towards the children, keen to join in the fun. Suddenly the child sat down with a thump and began to cry. Ambuya helped her to her feet and comforted her.

From time to time people engaged Ambuya in conversation as she sat there child minding. Today Chikomo joined her for a while; he sat down beside her.

'I need a rest, my arms ache. I have been mixing animal dung with earth and water, to make the plaster for the walls.'

'You find it hard work, my grandson.'

'Yes Ambuya, but it is work I enjoy. Soon the grass will be dry enough to harvest for the thatching. I see that Amai and the women have almost finished cutting down the *rapoko* and the mealies; they are nicely parched and shrivelled, ready for grinding.'

'There will be plenty of mealie meal this year. I expect Amai will use some of it to make the *sadza* for Usai's marriage feast. We shall need extra fish to dry and store for the celebrations, Chikomo.'

'Yes I know, Ambuya. I am going to spend more time fishing so there will be plenty of bream for the feast.'

Before the sun rose above the trees the following morning, Ambuya and Amai walked along the rows of harvested grain.

Other women did the same. Periodically Amai removed the sheaths from some of the maize cobs. 'These mealies are ready for grinding.'

'These too,' said Ambuya, ripping off the paper-like coverings to expose the dried grains beneath.

'I think it will be better to use freshly ground mealie meal for Usai's feast; he will bring us some bags of meal from the supermarket to replace what we use from our store.'

'The meal from the supermarket has a poor flavour,' said Ambuya, with distaste.

'I agree but it lasts a long time in the plastic bags and cannot be eaten by weevils.'

'That is true. There are still plenty of dried mopane worms in the store that can be used for the feast. We harvested more than usual last year; it took us many days to dry them on the *simbis.*'

'I intend to use some of them to make a pot of tasty relish,' said Amai.

The worms were the spiky green caterpillars of the emperor moth. Harvested from mopane trees during the hot dry season, they were sundried on metal discs to preserve them.

Using a knife, Amai began to strip the pale yellow grains from some maize cobs and put them into a deep wooden mortar. 'I will leave the *rapoko* to the younger women, Ambuya, those whose knees do not ache when they kneel down to do the grinding. Next year Neli will be here to help.'

'Yes and she will be able to take my place in the fields,' said Ambuya.

She walked slowly back to her rondavel and resumed her usual position on the blanket. Soon she was surrounded by small children. Picking up her crochet, Ambuya continued to work on the tablecloth.

Amai began to pound the grains in her wooden mortar.

'Let me help you Amai,' said Tabeth's mother.

'Thank you Ina, I would be glad of your help.'

Each of them used a long, round-ended pestle which they raised and lowered alternately, until the grains were crushed.

'I have noticed that Tabeth and Chikomo are showing an interest in each other, Ina.'

'Yes, I too have noticed.' The two women continued to work in silence for a while. 'Tabeth is a good daughter. I would miss her very much if she married a young man from another village.'

'You would like her to marry someone from our village? It is not the custom.'

'Our ancestors did not come from here; it would not be taboo. I would like Tabeth to remain close to me. Now that I have lost Pita, I do not wish to lose another child.' She walked away suddenly, her sorrow overwhelming her once more.

Amai put the crushed grains into a large, shallow winnowing basket and stood tossing it up into the air, shaking the outer chaff free so that it would blow away. Kneeling close to her, a young woman was grinding some tiny grains of millet on a granite stone. The grains were swiftly ground into fine brown *rapoko*.

'*Rapoko* porridge is my favourite,' said Amai, 'it has more flavour than mealie meal porridge.'

'I too prefer *rapoko*; I like it with plenty of sugar.'

After a time, Amai's crushed grains had been turned into coarse white mealie meal and her work was done, for now.

13

A faint glow appeared in the eastern sky, silhouetting the village. Outlines of people were visible, working around the cooking area where two large charcoal fires were burning. The goats that Usai and Mahachi had brought on their last visit were now skilfully butchered carcasses, skewered onto spits by Usai and Little Father.

'Let us lift the spits onto their props, Little Father.'

'The goats are heavy; they will provide us with plenty of meat.'

'Yes, and there is enough fat on the flesh to give it a good flavour.'

The sky became brighter, illuminating the area. The goats were now suspended directly over the centre of the charcoal fires. Hearing the sound of voices, some boys had crept out of their rondavels to watch.

'I need some volunteers to turn the spits,' Usai called to them.

The youths ran forward, eager to be chosen. Usai chose eight of the bigger, stronger boys.

'You must turn the spits slowly without a pause otherwise the meat will not cook evenly.' The boys watched as Usai demonstrated. 'Your arms will begin to ache after a time; you can take it in turns.'

The sun burst above the horizon into a cloudless cerulean sky, and suddenly the village was bustling with activity.

Close to the spits, in the regular cooking area, Mahachi

was busily preparing the chickens, cutting the plump breasts into pieces and placing them into his large cooking pot. Using a sharp knife he removed the tough, grey skin of a fresh pumpkin and cut the orange flesh into chunks, adding them to the other ingredients in the pot. Finally he sprinkled in the seasoning and herbs that would make a flavoursome sauce for the chicken to simmer in.

Next to him, Amai was putting fillets of bream, fresh onions and tomatoes into one of her pots and dried mopane worms and spinach into the other.

'Is that salt you are adding to your cooking pot, Mahachi?'

'Yes Amai, it is usual at the hotel to add salt to food when it is cooking, it improves the flavour.'

'I cook in the traditional way, without salt. I prefer to sprinkle it on to the food just before eating.'

'Would you like to add some of my herbs to your pot? I have many different kinds here in my bag; I picked them from the kitchen garden at the hotel.'

'I have not used herbs in my cooking before. Perhaps I will try a few.'

'Here, use these, they are good with fish.' He gave her some dill and parsley.

The pots were placed over the cooking fires and would simmer gently throughout the day, until the contents became thick and soup-like, forming a relish.

A group of women were sweeping the ground in the centre of the village, using besoms made from thin branches and twigs.

'We must make sure the village looks very smart for the celebrations,' said one of the women, as she skimmed the surface of the earth with her broom to make it smooth.

'Later, I will spread fresh blankets about the village for people to sit on.'

'The wood carvers are making a circle of stools, in front of the rondavel of our senior elder.'

'They are also putting seats and small tables over there under the trees, where Chikomo is working.'

Chikomo was busy unloading the barrels of Chibuku beer from Baba's old truck; beer that Mahachi and Usai had brought with them the night before. *Now that I am becoming a man*, thought Chikomo as he organised the bar area, *I should be allowed manly drinks, not the refreshing ones usually drunk by women and children*. His family, he knew, would have other ideas.

Ambuya stood outside her rondavel observing the activity around her. She bent down and unfolded two large pieces of paper that were lying on the ground. Inside each was a long length of traditionally woven material. The first was brightly coloured in shades of orange and yellow; the second was red and purple. She picked up one piece of material and shook it well, then folded it carefully and hung it on the back of her chair. *It is a while since Amai and I wore traditional dress*. She shook and folded the second piece of material. *The food smells good*. The aromas from the cooking were beginning to drift across the village.

By the time the sun had risen above the trees most of the villagers had completed their tasks. They were slowly making their way back to the rondavels to put on their traditional clothes and prepare for the occasion. As Mahachi strolled across the village he heard a raised voice speak his name.

'I see that Mahachi has been working in the cooking area, doing the chores of women. Could he not find man's work in the town?'

Mahachi stopped and looked in the direction of the voice. A group of maidens were walking towards the end of the village. Embarrassed by the comment, they all hid their faces; except one. She was looking at Mahachi, her mouth slightly upturned at the corners. He observed that the maiden was taller than the others, not one of the most beautiful but the movement of her body as she walked was enticing. She stopped for a moment and turned towards him, holding his gaze.

94

'I look forward to tasting your delicious chicken dish, Mahachi.' She laughed lightly.

Mahachi was surprised by her forwardness; it was not usual among maidens, yet there was something about her that attracted him, an indefinable quality. His eyes glanced briefly at her slim figure, her long shapely legs. He stopped suddenly, appalled by what he was doing. *It is not appropriate here in the village,* he silently reprimanded himself. He abruptly turned his back on the maiden and walked briskly away.

Ambuya chuckled as Mahachi walked towards her. 'She has been watching you for some time, my grandson. I told you on your last visit that she was a little too bold for some but she is still a fine maiden, is she not?'

'I do not recognise her Ambuya, what is her name?'

'Her name is Salomé. Her family has recently moved to the village; I am told they came from the west.'

Neli had spent the night at the chalet in town with her mother, Tandai, and her two sisters.

'Are you happy Neli?' her mother asked, as they drank tea together early the next morning.

'Yes I am. Usai and I love each other and we have a good life together.'

'Yet I see no sign that you are expecting a child, my daughter.'

'I have been using contraception; taking the pill.'

'Is that the wish of your husband?'

'No, he does not know.'

Neli's mother gasped.

'Mother, I had no wish to be pregnant before the traditional marriage, I might have suffered from sickness and that would have caused embarrassment to me and Usai's family.' In a placatory tone she added, 'I have stopped taking the pill now, mother, and I hope to conceive soon.'

'Let us hope that you do. People will begin to gossip if you do not, and Usai will become anxious. A barren wife is a serious matter. Usai is a good man, Neli. You are lucky to have a modern home and a husband with a well-paid job; there are many who would envy you. It is not enough to love Usai; you must respect him.'

Tandai loved Neli dearly but she did not always approve of her modern ways. She looked at her beautiful, wilful daughter. *By the end of this day you will belong to Amai, there could be dark times ahead for you both.* Tandai did not speak her thoughts aloud. She embraced her daughter lovingly.

'Make Usai happy, Neli. Give him many fine children and be a good daughter-in-law to Amai, it is your duty. Now we must get dressed. Your father will soon be here to drive us to the village.'

Usai stood outside the rondavel and looked about him. Groups of women were talking animatedly. Their lightly oiled arms and shoulders glistened in the sunlight and the brightly coloured traditional dresses and head-dresses made them look tall and stately.

The men were bare-chested and unshod; their oiled skins gleamed. From belts round their waists hung the tails of jackals and foxes; fur hats adorned their heads, animal skins decorated their arms and covered their shins.

Usai looked across at the boys turning the spits. They were chattering happily as they worked. The smell of succulent meat drifted towards him.

'How good the village looks today,' said Mahachi beside him.

Mahachi glanced across the village to where a group of maidens were standing. One in particular held his gaze. The statuesque figure of Salomé stood wearing her traditional skirt, tied round her waist like a sarong. He noticed that, unlike the girls and some of the maidens, she was not bare-breasted; she wore a translucent white blouse.

'Have you noticed how good the bar is looking Usai,' said Chikomo, coming out of the rondavel. 'I have been working very hard. There are plenty of chairs under the trees where the men can sit drinking beer. I thought I might join them for a while, later.'

'We shall see, little brother,' said Usai, smiling.

'They are coming,' shouted Chikomo, suddenly. 'I can hear the sound of motors.'

There was a buzz of excitement among the villagers. The first car came into view, followed by a convoy of other vehicles. They stopped and parked on the dirt road at the edge of the village. Doors opened and people stepped out. Villagers murmured among themselves.

'Look at the beautiful material of their clothes.'

'I like the dress that Neli is wearing.' It was the same one she had worn to the civil ceremony. This time she wore flat pumps on her feet.

'Some of the women are wearing wigs; see how shiny and straight the hair is.'

'The trousers and shirts of the men are very smart ...'

'... and expensive.'

Usai's face broke into a smile as he watched Neli and Khumalo coming towards him, followed by their family. He ran forward with Mahachi and Chikomo at his side. Leaping into the air, they twisted and turned as they danced a dance of welcome.

Behind them the villagers ululated, a continuous cry of joy.

14

Amai and Neli stood facing each other. Amai, tall and well rounded from child bearing, appeared regal in her traditional clothes of orange and yellow. Neli, taller and slimmer, looked beautiful in her modern dress of pink and lavender.

Neli gazed at the handsome face of her mother-in-law; it bore a strong resemblance to Usai's, the face she loved. She curtsied and shook Amai's extended hand, crossing her arms as she did so, as a sign of respect.

'I am very pleased to meet you Neli, welcome to our village,' said Amai. 'This is Ambuya, Usai's grandmother.' Neli shook her hand in the same respectful way. 'Come and sit with us, Neli, so that we can become acquainted.'

Ambuya and Amai sat on stools. Ambuya's was slightly higher. Neli chose to sit on a new colourful blanket that had been placed on the ground; tradition demanded that she must always sit lower than her mother-in-law.

'Usai told me that you work at the chemist shop in town. Do you work there every day?' enquired Amai.

'I do not work on Saturday afternoons and Sundays.'

'And do you have other free days, like Usai?'

'Yes, I am entitled to fifteen days holiday a year. I can take them whenever I choose.'

'Aaah,' said Amai and Ambuya in unison. They both nodded, satisfied with the reply.

Amai smiled at Neli. 'Would you like to fetch us some refreshing drinks?'

'Yes of course, Amai.' Neli stood up and walked towards the bar.

'I think Neli will do very well, Ambuya, she has plenty of free days to help me sow and reap.'

'Yes she has, you must hope that she will want to.'

'What do you mean?'

'I noticed that her fingernails are painted and I felt the softness of her hand when she shook mine; it was the hand of a woman who does not toil.'

'We will not think of such things today, Ambuya. We must be happy for Usai's sake.'

Neli returned carrying three orange drinks in small tumblers. She knelt down to serve Amai and Ambuya, as was the custom.

'Tell me about the chalet, Neli. Usai rarely speaks of it and I have not been there,' said Amai.

The two older women listened attentively as Neli talked. 'In the sitting room there is a sofa, two chairs and a coffee table. The kitchen has a small modern cooker and several cupboards. We have a table and chairs where we sit to eat our meals. The refrigerator is where we put our food to keep it fresh and Usai keeps his beer there to make it cold.'

'Aaah,' said Ambuya. 'What about a store room for mealie meal?'

'We use the cupboards to store mealie meal.'

'And where do you sleep?' asked Amai.

'We sleep on a comfortable bed, in the largest bedroom. There are wardrobes where we hang our clothes.'

She told them about the pink, purple and white petunias; the red hibiscus and the orange bougainvillaea Usai had planted in the front garden, to make it colourful. 'If you pay us a visit you can see for yourself how the chalet looks.'

'You have made it sound very attractive, Neli, but Ambuya and I rarely leave the village; it is not our way.'

'They are beginning,' interrupted Ambuya, pointing across the village.

Neli watched with interest as the elders began to congregate outside the rondavel of the senior elder, to begin the marriage ceremony.

The circle of stools arranged earlier by the wood carvers was now occupied by the village elders, including the *nganga*. Each wore a long cloak of animal skin tied at the neck with leather thongs; the ceremonial robe. Usai, Khumalo and Little Father were sitting with the elders. The marriage ceremony was now in progress.

'We understand, Little Father, that you conducted the marriage negotiations. Were they carried out to your satisfaction?' asked the senior elder.

'Yes elder, they were conducted according to our tradition, at the home of Khumalo.'

'Usai, were the negotiations for the *lobola* satisfactory?'

'I have agreed to pay Khumalo eighteen head of cattle.'

'Khumalo, has the *lobola* been paid in full?'

'We agreed that it would be paid over an unspecified period. I am satisfied with the two instalments which have been paid so far.'

'Why have you asked for cattle when we live in a tsetse fly zone? Where are the cattle to be kept?'

'The cattle will be added to my family herd, at our village in the south where there are no tsetse flies.'

The village elders sat for a while discussing the answers that had been given. When they were agreed that the negotiations had been carried out in an appropriate manner, the ceremony continued and Usai was asked to make his pledges.

The senior elder spoke. 'Usai, this village belongs to us all; the land is the property of our people and will be inherited by our children and grandchildren. Do you promise to maintain the customs and beliefs of our village and support those of us who remain here to protect it?'

'Yes elder. I will provide my family with whatever they require and make contributions to our village when necessary.'

'Will you observe the wishes of your mother, Amai, and send Nelisiwe to her when requested?'

'When Amai sends word, I will bring Nelisiwe here to help with the planting, and later to assist with the reaping of the harvest.'

'It is your duty to teach your children to understand the old traditions and to uphold the ways of our people.'

'I will bring my children here as often as possible, to spend time among you and to learn our beliefs.'

The elders discussed Usai's answers. When they were satisfied that Usai would honour his commitments, they stood up, indicating to all that the marriage had been solemnised and the celebrations could begin.

From opposite sides of the village, Usai and Neli walked towards each other and embraced, to the cheers and applause of the villagers. Their families gathered around them, shaking hands and laughing with pleasure.

'Welcome to our family, Neli,' said Amai, as she embraced her first daughter-in-law.

The rich harmonious voices of women filled the air, singing a song of joy to the newly married couple. The women, some in traditional dress others in modern, were moving in a single line, one behind the other. Clapping their hands rhythmically they danced slowly across the village towards Neli, encircling her. Their voices conveyed words of congratulations and wishes for happiness.

From the other side of the village, men moved towards Usai, gathering round him to dance. They stamped their feet and jumped vigorously into the air; their singing expressed hopes for good fortune and success.

The sound of a marimba could be heard; drums were being beaten, summoning young men and women to the centre of the village to perform a symbolic dance of fertility. Villagers, including Ambuya and Mahachi, surged towards the central area to watch.

Accompanied by the musicians the young women sang words of enticement; graceful shoulders swung from side to side, temptingly, curvaceous hips swayed provocatively to the tempo of the music.

The young men leapt excitedly into the air. They shuffled cautiously towards the young women, the motion of their bare torsos moving in time to the pulsating rhythm of the music. The young women retreated a short distance, coyly.

Mahachi's eyes were focused on Salomé, watching the movement of her hips and thighs.

The drumming grew louder and the pace increased each time the dance was repeated. Finally the drumming rose in crescendo, and the spectators cheered and applauded as the young women broke through the crowd and ran laughing around the village pursued by the young men.

'That reminded me of my youth,' said Ambuya to Mahachi, as the crowd began to disperse. 'I was already betrothed when I danced a fertility dance. Your grandfather was dancing with the young men. We were not allowed to touch, there were many people watching to see that we did not.'

Standing beside her, Mahachi made no comment. He was preoccupied.

The sun was now low in the sky; it was time for the feasting to begin. The bar area was piled high with boxes of canned and bottled drinks, and more barrels of Chibuku beer, contributed by Neli's family. Chikomo was working non-stop providing the women and young people with small plastic tumblers of Fanta orange or lemon. He was pouring beer into larger tumblers for the men. There was a buzz of merriment.

'Let me assist you, Chikomo,' said Mahachi, joining him behind the bar.

'I could do with some help. Suddenly everybody is hot and

thirsty, including me. When I have the time I will pour myself a tumbler of beer.'

Mahachi smiled. 'The men will consume a great deal of beer during the celebrations; they will be drinking far into the night. Later you will notice that some of them behave disgracefully. It will not be to the liking of Amai, neither will it impress Tabeth.'

Chikomo had not thought of that. He continued to work in silence for a while, considering Mahachi's words; he had no wish to disgrace himself in front of Tabeth.

'Perhaps it would be better if I drink Fanta as you do, Mahachi.'

Young people arrived to order drinks. Some were too thirsty to bother with tumblers and drank straight from the bottle or can. Suddenly, Salomé was standing in front of Mahachi, looking at him with her twinkling eyes.

'I would like a Fanta lemon,' she said.

As Mahachi stood pouring her drink she asked, 'Are there many men in the town who do cooking?'

'Yes. In the hotels all the cooking is done by men.'

She laughed. 'What do the women do?'

'They work in the laundry.'

Mahachi put the lemon drink in front of her. She picked it up and took a few sips, staring at him over the rim of the tumbler; as she did so the pupils of her eyes slowly dilated. Mahachi, willing his body not to respond, moved hastily away to serve somebody else.

'I am going to try some of your chicken now, Mahachi. I hope it tastes as good as our traditional food,' Salomé said as she walked away.

Mahachi ignored her.

'Her behaviour was disgraceful, wasn't it Mahachi?'

Mahachi grinned. 'Yes Chikomo, it was.'

Two bonfires had been built in clearings at the edge of the village. A pile of logs stood nearby.

103

'I am going to light the fires. Will you come with me Khumalo?' asked Little Father.

'Yes and I will find others to help us.'

'When the sun begins to sink, the strong smell of meat will attract hyenas, the scavengers.'

'We must find volunteers to keep the fires burning throughout the night.'

The sun had almost disappeared below the horizon, leaving just a glimmer of light. Two large fires were now burning brightly at the edge of the village. Oil lamps were positioned at intervals; they would be lit when darkness fell. People were sitting in groups on stools or blankets, some feasting on slices of goat meat, others on *sadza* and relish; they were drinking fizzy drinks or beer. There was an atmosphere of merriment everywhere.

Beyond the boundary of the village pairs of eyes could be seen reflecting the light from the fires; curious carnivores had come to investigate the smells, their mouths salivating from the aroma of the roasted flesh. Hyenas raised their snouts to sniff the air as they loped back and forth, keeping their distance from the bonfires. Black-backed jackals stood watching.

A musician began to play a tune on the marimba, using two wooden sticks. Drummers beat out a rhythm. People started to dance in the traditional way; men with men, women with women. Young and old together joined in the festive mood.

'I am having fun, Chikomo,' said Tabeth, as she watched the dancing.

'Me too,' said Chikomo. 'It is a while since we had a marriage in the village.'

'I hope my marriage will be as good as this one.'

'Has someone approached your father?' asked Chikomo, startled.

'Of course not, I have only just become a maiden.'

Chikomo was relieved.

Nearby, Usai and Neli were also watching the dancing.

'Perhaps we could leave the festivities soon and go to the rondavel without being noticed,' said Neli.

Usai laughed. 'We could try but I doubt that our departure would go unnoticed.'

They moved slowly away.

'*Manheru* Usai,' called out one of the men, chuckling.

'*Manheru* Neli,' said another.

There was a pause in the dancing as people turned towards them and wished them goodnight.

Neli and Usai giggled.

'You see,' he said.

A rondavel had been set aside for them in a quiet corner of the village. Inside, Usai took Neli in his arms. They held each other for a while without speaking.

'It would make me very happy if our first child was conceived here in the village where I was born.'

Neli pressed her cheek against his shoulder. 'Perhaps it will,' she said, as Usai's lips brushed the groove of her neck. She moaned softly.

Mahachi walked over to Ambuya, who was standing at the entrance to her rondavel.

'Are you thinking of going to bed, Ambuya?'

'I was, but the noise is still too loud for me to sleep. Let us sit and talk for a while, my grandson.'

Mahachi found a chair for Ambuya and a stool for himself.

'Ambuya, this morning you talked about the young woman called Salomé. You said she was a fine maiden. Why do you think so?'

'You do not like her?'

'I find her very attractive but she is unusually outspoken for a village maiden.'

'She has spoken to you?'

105

'She has spoken to me more than once, in a manner that her father would consider immodest.'

'She wishes you to notice her, Mahachi. She wants your eyes upon her, not on one of the prettier maidens.'

'You speak in her defence as though you admire her.'

'I like her for several reasons. One of them concerns you.' Ambuya looked at the handsome face and fine physique of her grandson. 'Mahachi, a time will come soon when you will want to marry. I am told there are very few shy, modest young women in the town; our village maidens would no longer please you, but Salomé might. Of course, it is possible that you find the maidens in town tempting and will choose to marry one of them, as Usai has done. But if Baba had not departed for the spirit world, you would have spent your life in our village and married a village maiden.'

Mahachi considered his grandmother's comments, surprised by the way she was often able to divine his thoughts. He wondered what else she admired about Salomé but he knew she would not tell him. She would leave him to discover that for himself.

'I will give some thought to your words Ambuya but I have no wish to marry at present. There are things I must do first.'

15

Three months had passed since Mahachi's last visit to Dr Meyer. It was now time for his next appointment. He sat in the waiting room recalling fragments of his liaison with Janacen, his reason for being here. He hoped that this would be his final visit.

'Mr Mahachi?' called the receptionist.

'Yes.'

'The doctor is ready to see you now.'

Mahachi knocked on the door of the surgery and walked in.

'Good morning Mahachi, do sit down.' Mahachi sat quietly, while the elderly grey-haired man quickly read through his medical notes. 'How have you been keeping?'

'I am feeling well, doctor. I have noticed none of the signs you described to me on my last visit.'

'No flu-like symptoms or feverishness?'

'No doctor.'

'Good. I am going to take another sample of blood from you. This will go to the laboratory as before. If the result is negative, it will mean that you are free from infection and you need not visit me again.'

As the doctor was withdrawing the blood from Mahachi's arm, Malachi noticed a series of small numbers tattooed on the doctor's wrist, and wondered why they were there. He was about to ask when the doctor spoke again.

'I will send the blood sample off today and you should

receive the results in a few weeks' time.' He pressed a small piece of cotton wool onto the tiny puncture mark.

'Thank you, doctor.'

Some weeks later, when a letter marked 'Confidential' arrived at reception for Mahachi, he put it into his pocket unopened. During the afternoon break he went to his bedroom and sat on the bed, looking at the envelope very anxiously. He slid his finger slowly along the flap and pulled out a sheet of typewritten paper.

'Negative ... Negative.'

He buried his face in the pillow on his bed and quietly wept.

At the village the following weekend, Mahachi sat talking to his grandmother.

'Salomé's father has not yet been approached,' said Ambuya. 'If you are interested in her you must not wait too long. She is unlikely to remain a maiden for much longer; some of her friends are already betrothed.'

From where he was sitting, Mahachi could see Salomé working with a group of young women. They were scrubbing some cooking pots with river sand, before standing them in the sun to dry. She was laughing and joking happily as she worked. When she had finished her chores she joined some of the older women. Sitting down beside them she listened respectfully to their instructions and Mahachi watched as she diligently practised the sewing skills they were teaching her.

Glancing at Mahachi, Ambuya noticed the direction of his gaze. 'I have heard rumours that young women in the town no longer learn craftwork; they cannot sew or crochet, so I am told. Here in the village, our maidens are still taught in the traditional way.'

Mahachi was silent for a while contemplating. 'Sometimes I go to the coffee bar on Main Street where young women sit gossiping. Some of their comments are full of contempt for the rural areas. I could not marry such a maiden.'

Ambuya's expression was inscrutable.

Later, Mahachi and Salomé met by chance as he was walking across the village. Her pace was leisurely and her slim hips moved sensually as she walked. Mahachi's heartbeat quickened as she approached.

'How long is your visit this time, Mahachi?'

'I will be leaving in the morning.' He felt a sudden urge to reach out and touch her.

'It is a short visit. You are keen to return to the town,' she teased.

'Perhaps.' He smiled.

Before he left the village, Mahachi spoke quietly to Ambuya. 'I would like you to send word, if anyone approaches Salomé's father.'

Ambuya nodded.

16

Mahachi now spent his spare time happily pondering the future; the idea of having a home of his own appealed to him. He indulged in daydreams about Salomé, trying to imagine the life they might share, in a small house not far from the hotel. The thought pleased him.

'Do you have a house in the Eastern Township?' Mahachi asked Mpofu, as they worked together in the hotel kitchen.

'Yes I do. My wife and children live there.'

'Did you buy the house or are you renting it?'

'I bought it.'

'How did you do that?'

'Like most of us I was unmarried when I first came to the hotel to work. With a room, free food and a uniform provided, I spent very little of my salary. In time I had enough money to buy a house in the township. I went to see an advisor at the building society.'

As Mahachi continued to work beside Mpofu he considered his own financial situation. A salary was paid into his account at the building society every month and apart from money he withdrew to help support his family, he spent only a small amount of it.

One afternoon the following week Mahachi walked across the road to the building society to enquire if he was eligible to buy a property in town and how to set about it.

* * *

110

'Shall we go and sit by the river?' said Usai.

'Yes, I have some things I want to talk to you about. Pleasant things,' Mahachi added, seeing the look of apprehension on his brother's face.

They found an empty seat and sat down.

'Usai, I am thinking of buying a house.'

'You are?'

'I have given some thought to your suggestion that I should marry. Now that my blood test has come back negative ....'

'Oh Mahachi, that is very good news.' Tears sprang to Usai's eyes as an image of Baba flashed across his mind; he brushed the tears away. 'I am so relieved.' It was a while before he could speak. 'Go on with what you were saying,' he said eventually.

'... I can begin to make plans. I have decided that when I marry I would like my wife to live in town, somewhere close to the hotel. I want you to come with me when I look at properties.'

'It will be a pleasure,' said Usai, smiling. 'May I ask if you have a young woman in mind to share this house with you?'

'Perhaps.'

'All right my brother, you can keep your secret for the present. I will meet you tomorrow afternoon at the estate agent and we shall see what they have for sale.'

The two brothers met several times during the next two weeks. Using Baba's old truck they visited several small houses in the Eastern Township, not far from the hotel. Each of them was much like the others, single storied and grey in colour.

'They are all so close together, Usai. I could never be happy in one of the houses we have seen.'

'Look at these,' said Usai, showing Mahachi pictures of two other properties the estate agent had given them. 'They are on the western side of town, near the Zambezi Drive, on the way to the village. They are small cottages in an isolated area. Shall we go and look at them?'

They drove along the small stretch of tarmac road that led to number three Mopane Close. It was in a cul-de-sac with many shady trees and just five other tiny cottages. Set in the centre of an oblong plot of bare earth, number three was surrounded by a hibiscus hedge with a metal gate in it. The outer walls of the cottage were painted pale terracotta; the clay tiles on the roof were a darker shade of the same colour.

They climbed out of the truck, opened the gate in the hedge and walked towards the cottage.

'I like it very much Usai. Let us look inside.'

They peered in through the windows.

'It looks very nice, Mahachi. The windows are a good size; the rooms will be light and airy.'

'The floors are dirty and the walls need to be painted but that is not a problem.'

'I could help you with the painting in my free time. I will bring Dorcas along to help with the cleaning.'

'How much does the cottage cost?'

'It is not expensive. You have enough money in your account to pay for it but you do not have sufficient to buy furniture as well. You will need a small bond, a loan from the building society.'

'Do you think I should buy the cottage?'

'I think it will be perfect for you.'

The interior of the empty cottage had a kitchen with cupboards and two gas rings. A short passageway led to two small bedrooms and a bathroom. The living room was long and full of light; windows overlooked the front and back garden. The cottage was cosy and secluded, and Mahachi felt very sophisticated now that he owned a property in town.

'I like your cottage very much,' said Neli, who had arrived

there one Sunday afternoon with refreshments for Mahachi, Usai and Dorcas. The two brothers had spent the weekend painting the walls white. Dorcas had been cleaning and polishing the floors.

'Are you planning to put plants in your garden, Mahachi?' asked Neli.

'When the next rains begin I am going to start a kitchen garden at the back. In the front I would like some colourful flowers like the ones around the swimming pool at the hotel. The hotel gardener says he will give me some seedlings.'

Usai interrupted their conversation. 'I forgot to tell you Mahachi, I visited the village last week.'

'Did you tell them about my cottage?'

'No, that is for you to do when you are ready. Ambuya gave me a message for you. I did not understand it but perhaps you will.'

'What was the message?'

'"Someone has approached her father."' Mahachi's heart began to pound. 'Do you know what Ambuya meant?'

'Yes Usai, I do.'

The next time he was free Mahachi spent the night at his cottage in Mopane Close, leaving the truck parked just inside the gate.

At dawn he dressed hastily, not bothering to eat breakfast. The early morning air was cool; he put on a thick sweater and set off for the village. The sunlight was just beginning to dance and flicker through the leaves on the trees when he drove into the village and parked the truck. Amai waved to him from the cooking area where she was making tea and preparing *rapoko* porridge. She was wearing a heavy jumper and a woollen hat. He walked over to her.

'That is just what I need, a dish of hot porridge.'

She laughed. 'I am glad to see you, my son.'

'Are you well Amai?'

'On cool mornings like this, my knees become stiff when I

bend down but otherwise I am fine. Come let us find Chikomo and Ambuya so that we can sit and talk.'

Ambuya, warmly wrapped in an old and shabby cardigan, said very little until she had finished drinking her mug of hot sweet tea. 'I need the sun to heat my old bones. How I dislike these cold mornings. Let us walk to the fields and back, Mahachi, the exercise will make me warm.' She held his arm and together they walked slowly across the village.

'Usai gave me your message. What has happened, Ambuya?'

'The father of a young man from the next village has approached Salomé's father, Josafat. The negotiations have only just begun; the *lobola* has not yet been discussed.'

'What can you tell me about this young man? Does he have a job in town?'

'Yes. I am told that he works as a gardener at the A'Zambezi River Lodge, where he lives in accommodation with other members of the staff. On his days off he returns to his village.'

'He has a car?'

'No, he has a bicycle.'

'I believe I have the advantage. As a chef I earn more money than a gardener and could afford to pay a larger *lobola*.'

'If you intend to make an offer for Salomé, you must speak to Little Father and ask him to begin negotiations for you, before it is too late. Now I would like to walk back to the rondavel, I need some hot porridge.'

Before Mahachi was prepared to seek Little Father's help, he wanted to be certain that somewhere within Salomé there was a genuine fondness for him; a promise of warmth and tenderness. It was during the hottest part of the day that the paths of Mahachi and Salomé crossed. She was walking with two of her friends; she looked gloomy and troubled.

'You are looking very miserable today, Salomé, quite different from when I last saw you,' Mahachi said.

114

'I *am* miserable,' she replied.

'Why is that?'

'Somebody from the next village has approached my father.'

'Congratulations! That is good news, surely.'

'But I do not want to marry a young man from the neighbouring village; I will have to live there.'

'That is the tradition, Salomé. Women are expected to live in the village of their husband.'

She spoke quietly, her voice sad. 'I had hoped to marry someone from our village.'

'Oh I see. Did you have anyone in mind?'

Salomé looked at him, her expression unusually vulnerable. 'I suppose that many of the young men who work in the town are not interested in village maidens,' she said resentfully.

'Those of us who work in urban areas see many pretty young women. Some are unchaperoned,' he said, looking at her two friends. 'What you say is quite possible.' He observed a look of disappointment on her face, but she quickly regained her composure.

'Do not let me detain you, Mahachi. I am sure you are anxious to return to the beautiful maidens in town.' She turned her back and walked away.

Mahachi smiled to himself. Before he left for town the following morning, he told the family about his cottage and expressed his wish to marry.

'Are you planning to marry someone in town, Mahachi, as Usai has done?'

'No, Amai. I am hoping to marry a maiden from our village but I have not yet approached her father.'

Amai embraced Mahachi, smiling delightedly.

'I know who she is,' said Chikomo, grinning. 'She is the one who behaved disgrace …'

'Hush,' interrupted Amai. 'We must wait until Mahachi is ready to tell us.'

'Now I must go and speak to Little Father,' said Mahachi.

Mahachi found him sitting on a stool in the sun. '*Mangwanani* Little Father, are you well?'

'*Mangwanani* Mahachi, yes I am well. I am also glad to see you. It is some time since your last visit.'

'Little Father, I need your help.'

'What is it?'

'I would like you to start marriage negotiations for me.'

'Who is the maiden you wish to marry?'

'Her name is Salomé. She and her family have recently moved to our village.'

'I know the young woman you mean but I understand her father has already been approached.'

'Yes Little Father, he has, but I am sure I can make him a better offer.'

17

Little Father was talking to Mahachi in a low voice. Mahachi sat listening intently.

'Josafat, Salomé's father, is keen for her to marry Jaya, a young man from the next village. I understand that a relative of his has a prospering business in the city and contributes many goats to their village. Jaya will be able to pay a handsome *lobola* for Salomé. I have persuaded Josafat to meet you before he makes a final decision, to hear what you have to say. I will ask him to see you before sunset today.'

'What advice can you give me, Little Father?'

'It is not for me to advise you. You are a fine young man with much to offer, it is for you to decide what you will say, but I can give you two pieces of news that were passed on to me by Ambuya. It is rumoured that the *lobola* being considered is eighteen goats. Also it seems that Salomé's mother has a fondness for trinkets.'

'Trinkets?'

'Yes. The beads that some women like to wear round their arms and necks. They can be bought in the Craft Village, Ambuya tells me.'

'Jewellery.' Mahachi pondered this news. He knew that Ambuya would not pass on such frivolous information unless it could be of use to him.

'I am going to the Hippo Pool for a while, Little Father, to think. I will be back before sunset.'

*　*　*

117

Inside Josafat's rondavel, the two older men shook hands.

'This is Mahachi, of whom I spoke,' said Little Father.

'*Masikati* Mahachi.'

'*Masikati* Josafat. I hope you are well,' said Mahachi, respectfully.

They shook hands.

'Sit down and let us talk,' said Josafat.

When the three of them were seated, Josafat spoke. 'Mahachi, Little Father tells me that you are interested in my daughter, Salomé. Jaya, a young man from the neighbouring village, has made me an offer for her which I intended to accept. At Little Father's request I have postponed my acceptance. What do you have to offer?' Josafat sat back in his chair ready to listen.

'Salomé would have a comfortable life with me, Josafat. The hotel pays me a good salary; a salary that contributes to the welfare of our village and its people.'

Josafat looked hard at Mahachi. It was a point well made.

'I am certain that I can exceed the *lobola* that Jaya has offered you. Also I have recently bought a small cottage in town where Salomé and I would live; the property would one day belong to your grandchildren.'

Mahachi watched Josafat as a look of self-satisfaction settled on his face.

'Mmm. A property in town for my grandchildren. Does my daughter know of this?'

'No she does not.'

'I doubt that living in town would please her, but that is not important. Continue with what you were saying.'

'Salomé would of course return to the village periodically and if she wished for some company at the cottage, her mother might like to pay us a visit. Salomé could take her shopping.'

'Shopping?'

'I have heard that there are shops in the Craft Village which are very popular with some of the village women.'

'Is that so?'

'I believe they sell beads that are worn decoratively.'

'Yes, so my wife has told me, often. A visit to the town would perhaps stop her endless complaining that she has nothing beautiful, while others have rows of bracelets on their arms and many fine necklaces to wear.' Josafat paused. 'Mahachi, my daughter was educated at a rural school; she has excellent skills that she has learnt from the village women. She is more spirited than the other maidens. I believe that this will be an asset to her if she is to adjust to life in the town. I would expect a *lobola* of twenty-five goats.'

Mahachi did not comment at first. He thought the price quite reasonable but he knew he would be expected to barter. 'I think your demand is excessive. I am already helping to support the village and have now provided a valuable asset for your grandchildren, not to mention a plan to keep your wife sweet-tempered. I am prepared to offer twenty goats.'

'I will accept nothing less than twenty-four.'

'Twenty-three.'

Josafat sat considering the offer. 'Very well,' he said finally. 'I will accept your offer of twenty-three goats but I would urge you to say nothing until I have sent word to Jaya that his offer has not been accepted.'

'As you wish, Josafat. I shall be returning to town early in the morning and will speak to Salomé on my next visit.'

Little Father watched as the two men shook hands.

Mahachi and Salomé walked across the village side by side. They were smiling at each other.

'Let us find a quiet place where we can talk,' said Mahachi. 'I have much to tell you, Salomé.'

Several villagers whispered as they passed. 'I am glad that Mahachi chose a village maiden, Amai will be pleased,' said one of them.

'Salomé is fortunate to have such a fine young man with a good job ...'

'... who is loyal to his family; he gave up his love of fishing to work in the town.'

The couple sat beneath the spreading ficus tree, their backs resting against its ample trunk. A few shrivelled wild figs littered the ground. Mahachi hesitated before speaking. In his mind he had a clear image of the future they would share together. He needed to lead Salomé step by step into her new life in the town, to make her feel at ease with the unfamiliar, unafraid of the sacrifices she would have to make when she became his wife.

'I have bought a cottage in the town.' He waited for her response but she looked at him, uncomprehending. 'It has several rooms, a garden and a hedge with a gate in it,' he continued.

'Tell me about the rooms, Mahachi. I have always lived in a rondavel.'

Mahachi painted a word picture of the place where they would live together, their home. Salomé sat with her eyes closed, listening to him.

'The cottage has a bathroom and two bedrooms; one is larger than the other. There are cupboards in the kitchen for storing food and two modern gas burners for cooking on. The living room has two windows; you can see the front garden from one and the back garden from the other.'

'Is there no furniture in the rooms?'

'Not yet.'

'Why do you want a cottage in town, Mahachi?' she asked, suddenly becoming curious.

'So that we can live there together after we are married in October.'

She sat up, frowning, finally understanding. 'You want me to live in the town?'

'Yes.'

'You are expecting me to leave the village, my family and friends, and live in a place where I would be among strangers?'

'I want us to live in the cottage together.'

'But I do not want to do that,' she said, becoming agitated. 'In my daydreams I imagined myself remaining here in the village and you visiting me whenever you were able. There are several women here whose husbands work in the town.'

'Salomé, I could not live such a life, I want my wife near me. But if you wish to remain here I will speak to your father, it may not be too late for you to marry Jaya.'

Salomé leaned back against the fig tree. She turned her head to look at Mahachi.

'I have loved you for a long time, Mahachi, even though you did not seem interested in me. I have no wish to marry Jaya; I want to be your wife and stay here in the village.'

'If you marry me you will have to live in the town. You will make new friends and we shall visit the village sometimes. In any case, you must be here when the rains begin to help Amai with the planting; you will see your family and friends then.'

They remained silent for a while.

'Maybe we could come here more often than "sometimes."' She smiled at him.

'Mahachi ... Mahachi?' Usai called. There was no sign of the old truck but the chain and padlock on the gate were hanging loose.

'I am in the main bedroom.'

'There is no truck outside.'

'I walked from the hotel.'

Usai wandered through the rooms looking at the spotless walls and polished floors, remembering how untidy the cottage had been when he and Mahachi had peeped in through the windows, for their first glimpse. 'You have almost finished painting I see,' he said, walking into the main bedroom. 'The cottage is looking clean and smart.'

'Yes, this is the last room I have to paint.' Mahachi climbed down from the ladder he was using. 'How the sound of our voices echo through these empty rooms.'

'They need some furniture.'

'But where can I buy it? There is none in town.'

'We will go together to the city in the south, to one of the wholesalers.'

'How will we transport the furniture to the cottage?'

'The wholesaler will send it in a large van.'

'Oh. So that is how it is done. How long does it take to arrive?'

'Normally three to four weeks.'

'Could we drive to the city the next time we are both free?'

'Yes, if you wish. It is a long journey; we will have to remain in the city overnight. I have friends we can stay with, guides that I trained with. But why are you in such a hurry to buy furniture?'

'I am betrothed.' Mahachi grinned.

Usai beamed and shook his brother's hand. 'That is wonderful news, Mahachi. Congratulations! Who is the young woman you are going to marry?'

'Salomé from the village.'

'Salomé. I hope she will make you very happy, although … I am surprised you did not choose someone from the town.'

'I want a wife who believes in the old traditions, who will not be troublesome when Amai sends for her to work in the fields.'

'Troublesome?'

'Yes. I have heard talk in the hotel kitchen that some women are refusing to go, when their mothers-in-law send for them.'

* * *

Usai opened the front door of his chalet. The smell of cooking drifted towards him, the evening meal was being prepared. He walked into the kitchen where Neli was busy at the stove.

'I have some good news,' he said.

'Tell me.'

'Mahachi is betrothed.'

'Oh. I am very happy for him. Who is he going to marry?'

'Salomé from the village. She is one of the maidens who danced at our marriage.'

'I remember her, she wore a white blouse.'

Usai walked to the kitchen window and stood for a while looking out. His mind wandered back to his conversation with Mahachi. 'Mahachi said something that puzzled me,' he said.

'What did he say?' asked Neli, as she began to stir mealie meal into a pot of boiling water, to make the *sadza*.

'He said that some urban women were refusing to help their mothers-in-law in the fields. Surely they must know the consequences of such an action?'

'Yes, I expect they do, but not everyone shares the same opinions.'

'What do you mean?'

'There are people in the towns and cities with jobs and professions; they have bought bungalows and land. Such people support their relatives in the villages, they send them money and provisions but they have no wish to visit the rural communities.'

'I am thankful that I have no such problems.' Usai waited for Neli to comment, but she remained silent.

It was September when the furniture was delivered to number three Mopane Close. Mahachi walked slowly from room to room admiring his purchases, remembering his visit to the wholesaler in the city.

'What about some fabrics?' one of the female assistants had asked him. 'Surely your wife will want to sew some curtains and soft furnishings, to beautify your home?'

'What do you suggest?'

'I can show you some attractive cotton material that has recently come in. I have several lengths of fabric that will tone very nicely with the colours of your new furniture. Also our clothes department has many pretty dresses in stock. If your wife is in need of new ones, you might like to take some along with you. Come, let me show you what we have.'

Mahachi had laughed at her temerity but before he left the wholesaler's, the assistant had persuaded him to buy several lengths of material as well as six dresses and a pair of sandals for Salomé.

He wandered into the living room and stood gazing out of the window at the back garden. He now had a small garden shed containing gardening tools. Just in front of the back hedge were two sturdy posts with a washing line.

The next time he was free, Mahachi drove to the village. The weather was hotter now; the bush south of the river was colourless and arid. The antelopes along the way looked leaner, their coats were lack-lustre. There was little nourishment in the grass they were eating. Troops of baboon were sitting on the ground, using their fingertips to search for dried seeds.

As Mahachi drove into the village a group of young men passed him, returning from the bush. On their heads they carried bundles of parched yellow grass. Mahachi climbed out of the truck and followed the boys who were walking towards the new rondavel; he was interested to see how the building was progressing. He found Chikomo sitting on the ground and sat down beside him.

'I see that the thatching is about to begin, Chikomo.'

'Yes there is plenty of dried grass in the bush now, ready to be harvested.'

124

Mahachi watched his brother for a while. Chikomo was selecting small bundles of the grass, which he trimmed to the same length and deftly bound together using strong, coarse grass. Tabeth sat close by, handing the blades of thicker grass to him when he needed them.

'You are becoming very skilled Chikomo, how neatly you tie and bind the grass.'

Chikomo smiled at his brother, glad to be praised. 'Soon I will be attaching these bundles to the roof poles, using strips of bark to hold them firmly in place.'

'Yes. I am familiar with the skills needed to build a rondavel, little brother.' Mahachi smiled, amused.

Chikomo grinned. 'This rondavel will be finished before your marriage. I think it will be set aside for you to use.'

Mahachi stood up. 'I will leave you to your work now Chikomo; I must find Salomé and tell her about the furniture I have purchased for the cottage. I will see you later.'

Mahachi was sitting with Salomé in the shade of the wild fig tree; the pale green leaves were interspersed with tiny pink blossoms. He was talking enthusiastically. 'The main bedroom now has a large comfortable bed, a wardrobe where we can hang our clothes and a wooden chest for storage.' He did not mention the dresses that were hanging in the wardrobe; he wanted them to be a surprise.

'What is being stored in the chest?'

'Various items, things we shall need later.'

'What items?'

'Mostly fabrics and sewing materials.'

Salomé giggled. 'You are planning to do some sewing?'

'No, you will be doing the sewing. Just a few curtains and cushions to make the cottage more attractive.'

'What if my needlework is poor?'

'Your sewing is good. I have seen the beautiful neat stitching you do when you sit gossiping with the women.'

'Tell me about the colours again, Mahachi.'

'The kitchen table and chairs are blue, paler than the sky. The colour of the three piece suite is called mustard; it is a yellow colour, like ripe mealies.'

'Are we going to grow flowers in our front garden? I have never grown flowers before although I have picked some in the wild.'

It was the first time that Salomé had said 'we' and 'our,' Mahachi observed. It made him feel warm inside.

18

The sun was now low in the sky. Slipping behind the trees along the river bank it cast a welcome shadow across the village, making the heat less intense.

Mahachi was standing with his grandmother watching the feasting and dancing at his own marriage celebrations. The smell of mopane worms frying in oil drifted towards them from the cooking area. Freshly harvested from mopane trees, the large green caterpillars being heaped onto plates were fat and juicy.

Salomé was dancing in the centre of the village with the women. Mahachi and Ambuya watched her graceful movements.

'Your wife is looking very beautiful today, in her traditional dress and head-dress.' Ambuya smiled. 'She has loved you for a long time and it pleases me that you are now married. She will look after you well and you will grow to love her in time.'

Puzzled by the comment, Mahachi stared at his grandmother. 'But Ambuya, I love her now. We are very happy together.'

'I have noticed your fondness for her but your face does not yet show the signs.'

'Your words surprise me, grandmother, I do not understand them.'

'You will in time, my grandson.'

Nearby, Amai and Neli were sitting together, talking.

'I have heard that fine soaps and lotions are sold at the

chemist shop, ones which are made especially for women and have a beautiful perfume. Is this true, Neli?'

Neli smiled. 'Yes Amai, it is true. I use them myself. The scent from the soap lingers on the skin and gives it a pleasant smell. Also, I use lotion at this time of year when my skin becomes dry.'

'I have always used the plain soap, bought at the supermarket, and I put oil on my skin during the dry season, but I am interested in the fine products you sell.'

'I will give some to Usai to bring to you on his next visit. You can decide whether or not you like them. If you do, I will send you some more.'

Amai smiled with satisfaction. It was useful having such a daughter-in-law. 'That is kind of you Neli, but there is no need to give them to Usai, you can bring them yourself when the rains begin.'

Neli stared at Amai and her lips parted as if she intended to comment, but Amai's warm friendly smile was disarming and Neli lowered her eyes. Her words remained unspoken.

At the bar area in a shady corner of the village, Usai and Chikomo were working together serving drinks.

'The weather is hotter than it was at your marriage, Usai. People are very thirsty today and are drinking much more.'

'October is always the hottest month,' said Usai, gulping Chibuku beer from a tumbler, in between serving people drinks.

Chikomo watched him with envy. 'I wanted to drink some beer at your marriage but Mahachi said people behave disgracefully when they drink beer. Yet you are drinking it.'

'I drink very little Chibuku, most of the time I drink Coca Cola.'

'I would like to try some beer,' Chikomo persisted.

'You are still too young. Amai would not approve.' He saw the look of disappointment on his youngest brother's face and decided to capitulate. 'I have an idea. We could compromise, just this once. You must promise not to tell Amai.'

'I promise, I promise.'

'There is a drink called shandy. It is made mostly from lemonade but there is some beer mixed with it. Some of my tourists find it tasty and refreshing.'

Usai put a small amount of Chibuku beer into a plastic tumbler and filled it with lemonade. He handed it to Chikomo, who took a sip.

'This is delicious. Thank you, Usai, thank you.' He took a long gulp. 'Mmm, shandy. Perhaps …'

'No Chikomo,' said Usai, divining his brother's thoughts. 'you can have only one. If you drink more, Amai will notice the smell of beer about you.'

Two days after the marriage ceremony Mahachi left the village and set off for town, eager to return to his cottage. He drove slowly along Mopane Close when he reached it, so that Salomé could admire her new surroundings.

Inside the cottage he led her into the living room. The walls were now brilliant white and the concrete floors gleamed with wax polish. The pristine three-piece suite stood in the centre of the room. In front of it, standing on a colourful patterned rug of yellow, orange and brown, was a large coffee table. A nest of tables stood beside the sofa.

'This is even more beautiful than I imagined, Mahachi.' She sat on the sofa and bounced up and down. 'It is so soft.'

'Yes, you will be able to sit very comfortably when you are doing some sewing. Come. Let me show you the other rooms.'

Salomé peeped inside the wardrobe of the main bedroom. 'Whose dresses are these?' she asked.

'They belong to my wife.'

Salomé stared at Mahachi for a while, her expression blank. Suddenly understanding, she laughed delightedly.

'They are for me! Thank you Mahachi, I am going to try them on.'

'You can do that later,' he said, shutting the wardrobe door.

On the night of their marriage, in the darkness of the new rondavel, the noise of the celebrations and the proximity of the villagers had inhibited Mahachi. Used to his own room at the hotel and the quiet solitude of the cottage, he had felt uncomfortable. Yet his longing for Salomé had been so great, he had taken her impatiently without consideration. Now, in the seclusion of their cottage and the comfort of a soft bed, he could give her the pleasure that her body had kept secret from her.

He undid the buttons of her blouse. Beneath it, her dark velvety skin was flawless, her small breasts firm. His hand brushed across her rich brown nipples as he slipped the blouse off her shoulders. He untied her skirt and let it fall to the ground, revealing the shapely curves of her narrow waist, her smooth sensual hips and thighs.

On the bed he gently kissed her body. Barely touching her skin with his lips he felt the gooseflesh form. His skilful hands explored her; he watched her face change with each new sensation, listened to her breathing quicken.

He entered her urgently, feeling the hot moisture envelop him. When her gasps became cries, he lost all control and his body erupted into a burst of intense pleasure.

Mahachi had taken some leave so that he and Salomé could spend a week alone together. In spite of the increasing October heat they made love often. Afterwards they soaked languidly in the bath.

Sometimes in the cool of early morning they walked through the rainforest, the damp spray from The Falls drifting over them like a tepid shower. On other occasions they would wander beneath the shady trees, along the river path.

'I would like you to show me how to cook some of the dishes you make at the hotel, Mahachi. My traditional cooking will no longer please you now that you are used to different food,' Salomé said one day.

After sunset, when the air was cooler, they worked together in their kitchen to produce the evening meal. Salomé stood at the kitchen table, slowly peeling and chopping onions.

'Hurry up with those onions, this oil is ready for frying them.'

'I cannot work as fast as you Mahachi, I am doing my best.'

He moved to the table to help her. Taking the knife from her hand and using swift skilful movements, the onions were soon neatly sliced.

'How quickly you work. I wish I could do the same.'

'You will improve with practice. In any case, I still enjoy traditional food.'

When the meal was ready they sat down at the blue kitchen table to eat.

'This is one of the meals we cook at the hotel for vegetarians; the people who do not eat meat or fish. Do you like it?'

Salomé took a mouthful of food. 'Mmm. It is very tasty, Mahachi. I enjoy eating rice instead of *sadza* and the tomato sauce you have mixed with the vegetables is delicious.'

They ate in silence for a while. Mahachi was reflecting on his imminent return to work. 'I notice that you have not yet looked inside the chest.'

'Maybe tomorrow I will take a look.'

'I would prefer you to do it today.'

Later, in the bedroom, he said, 'Open the chest Salomé and see what is in there. Go ahead.'

Salomé lifted the heavy wooden lid and peered inside. She saw that the chest was full of parcels. She took several of them out and unwrapped the paper, spreading the contents on the bed. The bed became a riot of colours, covered in lengths of fabric in many shades and hues. She picked up some blue patterened material which she took into the kitchen.

'Look. This is the same colour as the table and chairs.'

Mahachi stood beside her, smiling. She went back into the bedroom and selected some yellow and orange material. Taking it into the living room, she draped the fabric across the back of the sofa. 'This material matches the other colours in the room. I can make curtains for the windows and maybe some cushions, if there is enough cloth.'

Standing close to her, Mahachi silently thanked the female assistant at the wholesaler for her good taste. 'Come and sit beside me, here on the sofa. I need to talk to you.'

Salomé looked at him apprehensively as she sat down. 'I hope you are not going to tell me something unpleasant.'

'I have to return to work tomorrow.'

She looked disappointed. Clasping his hand she said, 'Being together has made me very happy, must you go back so soon?'

'Yes Salomé, I must and there is something else. In addition to the meals I prepare for our guests at the hotel, I also have extra duties to do. Sometimes I am on an early shift, preparing food for the white-water rafters to take with them. At other times I am on duty at night, in case any of the guests want room service. That is why I am a resident chef. It means I must live at the hotel.'

'But now you have a home, you no longer need to live there.'

'Yes I do; it is part of my contract. I will be home whenever I am free, sometimes during the day, at other times for the night.'

'You mean I am to be left here alone with no one to talk to? What will I do all day?'

'You will be busy keeping our home clean, and now you have plenty of material to do some sewing. During the rainy season you will be able to grow vegetables and plant mealies in the back garden. I will bring you some seedlings from the hotel nursery.'

'I did not expect this. I was looking forward to seeing you every day. And besides, how am I going to become pregnant in time for the rains, if I must spend the nights without my husband?'

'Why must you be pregnant in time for the rains?'

'Imagine the shame if I am not. When I return to the village for the planting people will expect it. "When is your baby due?" my friends will ask.' Imitating her father's baritone voice she said, '"I hope you are being a good wife to Mahachi. You are lucky to have such a fine husband."'

Mahachi laughed at her mimicry. 'I will do everything I can to make you pregnant before you see your friends again.' He gently nibbled the groove of her neck. 'Promise me that when I am away you will lock the doors and padlock the gate every night.'

19

Mahachi opened the gate and walked along the driveway to his cottage. Through the living room window he could see Salomé standing on a chair; she was hanging a curtain that she had painstakingly hand-sewn. He stood watching her for a while unnoticed as she smoothed the yellow and orange fabric, singing to herself as she admired the effect of her handiwork.

He loved her.

The realisation came as a surprise to him. His fondness for her at the time of their betrothal had grown into something much stronger. He could no longer imagine his life without her. He opened the front door and walked across the room to where she was standing. She looked down at him and smiled.

Yes, he loved her.

'This is the first of the few curtains and cushions I am going to sew, to make our cottage more attractive,' she said. 'What do you think of it?'

Mahachi laughed as she quoted his words from the past. 'I think it is very fine.'

'How long can you stay?'

He gazed at her, glad that she was his.

'Are you going to tell me or must I guess?' she asked, as she stepped down from the chair.

'For two nights.' He enfolded her in his arms and held her close.

'You are pleased to see me.' She nestled against him. 'You did not use the truck today; you must be hot after your walk from the hotel. Shall I fetch us some cold drinks?'

'Yes, I would like some Fanta orange.' He sat down on the sofa.

'I hope it will rain soon and make the air cooler,' she called from the kitchen, as she took a large bottle out of the refrigerator and filled two glasses.

'Then Amai will send for you and I will have to take you to the village to stay for a while,' he said, as she came back into the room.

'Will you miss me?' she asked, handing him one of the glasses and sitting down beside him on the sofa.

'Not at all,' he joked. 'I plan to spend the time drinking at the beer hall with my friends. I may even go to the city and drink with Usai's friends.'

'How can you say such a thing,' she said, laughing, playfully pummelling his chest with her fist. 'Maybe I should have married Jaya after all.'

'I am glad that you did not.'

She saw the love in his eyes, for the first time. 'I had a visitor yesterday,' she said.

'Did you?'

'Yes. The young woman who lives at number five came to see me, to welcome me to the Close she said, but I think she was lonely. She told me that her husband works in the south; she only sees him on public holidays and when he takes his annual leave.'

'I told you when we sat beneath the fig tree in the village that you would make new friends.'

'Yes I remember.'

'In time you will make other acquaintances in the neighbourhood.'

He smiled at her, happy they would be together always.

'While you are away helping Amai, I will start to make our

135

garden. I am going to plant pumpkins and mealie seeds in the back garden and maybe some shrubs at the front.'

'I would like some busy lizzies.'

'Would you?'

'When I return from the village I want to plant some along the driveway so that when we open the gate there are beautiful flowers to greet us.'

When the sun disappeared behind the horizon and the heat was less intense, Mahachi unpacked the food that he had brought with him from the hotel and set it on the kitchen table.

'What food have you brought for us to eat?'

'Rice, chicken with peanut butter relish and some small fruit tarts,' he said.

They sat down to eat. After a few mouthfuls Salomé pushed her plate away.

'What is the matter?' he asked. 'Do you not like the food?'

'I am not feeling hungry.'

Outside, the leaves on the trees began to rustle as they brushed against each other. A gentle breeze blew in through the open windows making the single curtain billow into the living room. In the distance a flash of bright light lit up the dark sky. A clap of thunder followed, the first of the season. A brisk wind began to blow. Mahachi and Salomé stood at the kitchen window watching, as the first droplets of water hit the bare soil. Soon the drops became a downpour and the air was filled with the smell of damp earth.

They went outside and stood on the doorstep their faces raised to the sky, letting the refreshing rain wash over their heads and run down their bodies, drenching their clothes. They laughed with pleasure, their arms outstretched to embrace the giver of life.

20

In the chalet Usai was sitting in an armchair, browsing through a wildlife magazine. He raised his eyes and gazed out of the window for a while, watching the rain slowly subside. The first storm of the season was almost over. He looked across at Neli who was sitting on the sofa.

'Now the rains have begun,' he said, 'it will not be long before Amai sends for you and Salomé.'

Neli laughed. 'Usai, I have no intention of going to the fields to help with the hoeing and planting. I am an urban dweller; I have a job.'

He stared at her, infuriated by her disloyalty. 'Of course you will go; you are my wife, you have no choice. I made a pledge to the village elders at our marriage ceremony.'

'But Usai, there are many women living in towns and cities who do not go nowadays. They support their relatives, of course, but they have no interest in the communal areas. Some women live hundreds of kilometres from their mother-in-law's village; they have no wish to make such a long and difficult journey.'

'The village is only twenty kilometres from here. You cannot use distance as an excuse, apart from which I have no interest in the views of other women.' Usai's eyes glinted with anger.

'You can use our money to provide Amai and the family with anything they need, but I will not go to the fields,' she said emphatically.

Usai glared at her. 'I shall be away for the next four days. While I am gone I want you to pay a visit to your mother, to ask her advice. I am sure she will explain what is expected of you.'

'Where are you going?'

'National Parks have asked me to take a group of backpackers south to the game reserve.'

Usai set off early the following morning to collect an open-topped Land Cruiser from the National Parks office. He hoped that when he returned home his problem with Neli would be resolved. He drove to the centre of town to collect the six young tourists.

'Good morning,' he said, 'I am Usai.' He shook each of them by the hand.

'Morning.'

They climbed on board and threw their backpacks under the bench seats. Usai drove along Main Street and took the route south. It was lined with tall trees which formed an archway over the tarmac road, shading them from the scorching November sunshine. Sitting in the open vehicle a welcome breeze blew onto their faces. The tourists were talkative and full of excitement.

Leaving the road, Usai turned right onto a narrow dirt track and into the bush. Just ahead of them, grazing in an area of open grassland, was an unusually large herd of impala. They turned their heads inquisitively as the vehicle approached. Usai braked suddenly, reversed several feet and switched off the engine.

'There is a female leopard crouching at the side of that large bush,' he said, pointing.

The group murmured and stood up for a better view. All at once the predator made her move; she sprang out of her hiding place and launched herself at one of the smaller antelopes. The young impala zigzagged speedily away, out of reach; the leopard was left standing. The cameras clicked.

The herd of impala turned to face their enemy. Some of them began to make staccato barking sounds. Others joined in, eventually the whole herd. The leopard crawled out of sight into an area of thicket.

'She will remain hidden until the herd settles down, then she will attack again,' Usai explained.

The noise from the herd attracted a spotted hyena that loped towards them across the bush. It sniffed around the shrubbery where the leopard was hiding and lay down nearby, to wait.

'If the leopard makes a kill the hyena will attempt to steal her prey,' explained Usai. 'The hyena is a powerful scavenger.'

As the group continued to observe the thicket, it seemed that the leopard knew she was outmatched; she retreated from the back of the bushes and disappeared from view. The noise stopped. The impala resumed their grazing, the hyena fell asleep.

'Wow! That was something else,' said one of the tourists.

Usai started the engine and drove on. 'Yes, it was a good start to our safari. It is rare to see a leopard hunting during the day. Let us hope our afternoon drive will be as good.'

He had been exhilarated by the sight of the big cat. As he had watched her sleek body in motion and her violent intentions thwarted, he felt his heart beat faster and the adrenalin flow. This was his element, his great passion: the untamed bush.

They reached Kudu Camp, their destination, at midday; the smiling warden was at the entrance waiting to greet them.

Kudu Camp was situated beneath an area of thick shady woodland, deep in the bush. Periodically the sunlight flickered through the trees onto ten thatched lodges. All around, the buffalo grass with its broad flat blades was well watered and green. Usai loved staying at this calm sanctuary.

That afternoon, on the elevated platform at *Mhuka* Pan,

the group sat on folding wooden chairs. The large pan had many markings in the mud made by hooves and mighty foot-pads.

'What does *Mhuka* mean?' asked one of the tourists.

'It means wild animals; large numbers come here to drink. Would anyone like a beer?' Usai enquired. They all laughed and raised their hands.

'I should say, in this heat.'

Removing the lid of the cool-box he had brought with him from the camp, Usai opened the bottles of chilled Castle beer and handed them out. The group sat silently sipping their drinks, waiting.

'There,' said Usai suddenly, 'elephant.' He pointed to an area of dense bush on the other side of the pan. A single female elephant had broken cover. Two more silently joined her. 'They are checking for danger,' he whispered.

The herd gathered soundlessly behind the matriarchs. All at once the elephants moved swiftly forward. The tourists whispered to each other, their voices full of enthusiasm; the cameras clicked and whirred. The herd, with two young calves and one new-born, entered the water.

'The new-born will still be feeding on its mother's milk; it will not drink the water. It has not yet learnt to use its trunk,' explained Usai, quietly.

He watched the tiny elephant child, its mother close by to help and protect it. *How I long for a child of my own*, he thought, *a son to pass on my love of the wild, or a daughter who looks like Neli. Why has she not conceived? It is now six months since the civil marriage.*

He came out of his daydream when the group burst into laughter; they were watching the calves wallowing playfully.

That night, as Usai lay alone in bed, Mahachi's words drifted into his mind: *I want a wife who will not be troublesome ...* As he became drowsy he thought of Neli. He missed her comforting body beside him. He hoped that she loved him enough to make the right decision.

Not far away, two male lions could be heard communicating with each other. Their fearful roars were the last sounds he heard before falling asleep.

Usai lay soaking in the bath at home in the chalet. The early morning game drive and the return journey had made him dusty. He closed his eyes and relaxed in the tepid water, revisiting his stay at Kudu Camp; the pleasant company, the wildlife and the tranquillity. He heard the sound of the front door open.

'Are you home, Usai?' called Neli.

'I am in the bathroom.' He stood up, dried himself and went to join her. He found her in the kitchen, lifting some heavy bags of shopping onto the table.

She smiled brightly at him. 'I am glad that you are home, I have missed you.' She put her arms round him and hugged him. He held her tightly; for a moment all problems between them were forgotten.

'I am going to cook a special meal for us; chicken and sweet potatoes,' she said, as she unpacked the shopping bags. 'Tell me about your trip while I prepare the food.'

Usai took a cold drink out of the refrigerator and sat down at the kitchen table. 'I really enjoyed working in the bush again. We saw so much wildlife drinking at the pans; the riverbeds are still dry and the streams are not yet flowing.' His words triggered in him thoughts of the main rains to come. He took a gulp of his cool drink. 'Tell me about the visit to your mother.'

Neli sighed. 'My mother agreed with you.'

'What did she say?'

'She told me that when she was young she travelled far to the south to help her mother-in-law. The journey was long and difficult but my father insisted it was her duty. She said it

141

was the same for me. I should be a dutiful wife and do as my husband wishes.' Neli paused. 'But my mother was not well educated; she did not have a job. It is different for me.'

'You are going to disregard your mother's advice?' asked Usai, shocked.

'Yes. Many of my friends in the township do not help in the fields. Their husbands are not concerned, they are also urban people. They have little interest in the rural communities.'

He stood up and walked towards her. 'I was raised in a village. *I* am concerned,' he said, angrily. 'Surely your mother told you there could be repercussions.'

'She told me there could be unpleasant consequences but my friends tell me many villages are adjusting to the ways of young people.'

'It seems that you spent a good deal of time listening to the advice of your friends. I doubt that my village would agree with their opinions. It occurs to me that this is not the first time the young people in the township have influenced you.'

Neli stopped working. 'What do you mean?'

'We have been married for six months Neli, but you have not yet conceived. Can you think of any reason why that should be?'

Neli lowered her eyes, unable to look at him. She did not answer.

'Do you recall a conversation we had soon after the civil ceremony, when you told me about the Family Planning Clinic in the township? You said that some people were choosing to have small families?'

Neli still did not speak.

'Answer me!' said Usai, his voice raised.

'Yes I remember,' she said. She sat down, her eyes still downcast.

'Have you used the clinic?'

'Yes I have.'

142

'In spite of the views I expressed at the time?'

'Yes, but I no longer go there.'

Usai stared at Neli in disbelief, astonished by her deceit. 'So, not only have you used contraception, contrary to my wishes, but in addition you intend to ignore Amai's request for help.'

He raised his hand and struck her forcefully across the face. He heard her sharp intake of breath. She raised her face to look at him, her eyes filled with tears.

'When Amai sends for you, you will obey your husband and both our families.'

21

Usai's lovemaking lost its tenderness. The warmth between him and Neli, the loving gestures they shared, diminished and finally stopped. Their coupling fulfilled his needs; he no longer considered hers. In bed he would sometimes hear her weeping quietly, before she fell asleep.

Yet during their frequent arguments Neli remained adamant. She stubbornly refused to agree to the one thing that would repair the damage to their rapidly deteriorating relationship.

When the storms became more frequent and the rain torrential, they rarely spoke to each other. The tension between them mounted as they waited for Amai to send word.

One evening, Usai came home with a letter in his hand. He sat down beside Neli on the sofa. 'This was handed to me today when I checked in at the office. It is from Amai. She needs you at the village,' he said.

Neli leaned forward. Resting her elbows on her knees, she covered her face with her hands. 'I have not changed my mind, Usai. I will not be going,' she said, her voice weary from their disagreements.

'You are prepared for the consequences?'

She shrugged.

He stood up abruptly. 'I am going to see Mahachi, to give him the message from Amai. When he takes Salomé to the village at the weekend I shall go too. I must explain your absence to my mother.'

144

Neli remained silent.

Usai walked to the front door and turned to look at her, his face was distorted with fury. He slammed the door behind him as he left.

'I did not think Neli would come,' said Amai, as she and Usai sat together at the village. 'When I saw her at the traditional marriage, her clothes and make-up told me that she belonged to the urban life. There are many young people nowadays who have no wish to dirty their hands with the soil that feeds them. It is a great pity. We need Neli here. Ambuya is too old now to hoe and reap and I do not work as fast as the young.' She looked at Usai, her first-born, 'I feel a great sadness for you, my son. If only ...'

'If only what?'

'I was thinking of Chipo. I hoped you would marry her, she shared our beliefs in the traditional life.'

Usai lowered his eyes. He had disappointed his mother and he felt ashamed.

'You must speak to Little Father, Usai. Ask his advice.'

He strolled across the village to Little Father's rondavel. An outburst of laughter drew his attention. He turned and saw Mahachi and Salomé with a group of young people, talking animatedly to them. Usai felt a wave of jealously pass through him; he quickly suppressed it. He loved his brother, he wanted Mahachi to have the happiness that was slipping away from himself and Neli.

'May I speak to you Little Father?'

'Sit down beside me, I have been expecting you. It is rumoured that Neli is refusing to help Amai. Is this true?'

'Yes, Little Father, it is. I have talked to her on many occasions but she will not come.'

Little Father sighed. 'It is a serious matter. You have broken your pledge to the elders and your wife has ignored and insulted her mother-in-law.'

145

'What will happen?'

'If Neli does not come to the village for the reaping, the elders will insist that Amai bans you from the village.'

'Would I be permitted to visit my family?'

'No, such a meeting would not be tolerated by the elders.'

'When the time comes, I would hope to attend Chikomo's marriage ceremony.'

'Usai, you would not be permitted to come here at all, even for such an important occasion.'

'But this is where I was born.'

Little Father's expression was full of pity when he looked at Usai and saw the dreadful anguish on his face. Neither of them spoke for some time.

'There is an alternative, though it may not be to your liking.'

'What is it, Little Father?'

'You and Neli must separate. You will not be banned if Neli is no longer your traditional wife.' Little Father paused. 'I understand that Neli has not yet conceived. A barren wife is unacceptable. If she cannot give you a child, you are entitled to approach her father, Khumalo. He would be compelled to return your *lobola* and take her back into his family, disgraced.'

Usai wished to hear no more. He stood up. 'Little Father, I need to consider your words.' He called out to his brother. 'Mahachi, come!' Usai walked out of the village and hurried towards the Hippo Pool.

Mahachi found him sitting on the river bank hugging his knees, deeply distressed. Mahachi sat down beside him and put his arm round his brother's shoulders to comfort him.

When Usai returned to the chalet the following afternoon he found Neli lying on the bed, resting. She was home earlier than usual. Usai felt a sudden flash of anger towards her, the desire to hit her, beat her. Turning his back on her he walked

146

towards the window, his shoulders hunched, his stomach tense.

'I need to talk to you, Neli, to explain the choices I have available to me; my decision will determine our future. Do you realise the trouble you are causing me and my family,' he said angrily. 'In time your family will be affected too.'

'I am expecting a child,' she whispered.

Usai turned to look at her. 'What did you say?'

'I am pregnant.' She smiled at him.

'Are you sure?'

'Yes, I visited Dr Meyer today. He said our baby will be born after the rains.'

Maybe our problems will resolve themselves. Usai felt the tension leave his stomach, his shoulders relaxed.

His smile was tentative at first; it grew into an enormous grin. 'A child, this is wonderful news Neli.' He sat down on the bed close to her. 'You will be able to give up your job and be a mother; raise our first-born. You can spend some time in the village with Amai, how glad she will be …'

Neli interrupted him. 'No Usai. That is not what is going to happen.'

'What do you mean?'

'The chemist has agreed to give me some leave when the baby is due. I plan to go back to work later. I am going to hire a young girl from the township to look after our child. I want her to live here.'

'You are planning to hire a nanny?' said Usai, aghast.

'Yes, that is what I intend to do.'

'You are forgetting that the chalet belongs to me, it was bought long before we met. It is our home but my chalet,' he said emphatically. 'I will not permit a nanny to live here. It is for you to look after our child.'

'Then I will hire her to come in daily on the bus, to look after the baby while I am at work. Usai, we are living in an emerging country, we need to do the most we can for our children. With two salaries we can give them a better future, provide them with the best education.'

'I already plan to give my children a good life and even if I agreed with your reason for continuing to work, there remains the unsolved problem between you and Amai.'

'I will never agree to work in the fields, Usai. I want an urban life and no other.'

Usai stormed out of the bedroom shaking with fury. Only Neli's pregnancy prevented him from striking her. He walked into the kitchen, his fists clenching and unclenching. Taking a bottle of beer out of the refrigerator, he removed the cap and took a long gulp. As his tension eased and he became calmer, snippets of a previous conversation between himself and Neli flashed across his mind.

'*Large families have more mouths to feed; small families have more money,*' Neli had said.

'*How big is a small family?*'

'*It is usually two children,*' she had replied.

He began to understand Neli's intentions and comprehend the depth of her determination. He knew then that his marriage to her had been misguided.

When a vacancy at National Parks became available and Usai was offered the job, he was delighted and relieved. It would give him the opportunity to work permanently at Kudu Camp, his favourite bush camp. It would also enable him to spend time away from Neli, to put some distance between them.

'National Parks have offered me a post working regularly at Kudu Camp. I have accepted the position,' Usai told Neli one evening.

'Will you be away often?' she asked.

'I will be there from Saturday to Wednesday every week, then I have two days free.'

'So I will only see you for a few hours each week.'

She sounded disappointed but Usai did not comment.

In his mind a plan began to take shape, one that would ultimately bring him peace if not happiness. He would discuss it with Little Father the next time he visited the village.

22

'Am I too young to marry?'

Amai looked at Chikomo, amused. 'Not too young but it would be unwise at this time.'

'Do you think so?'

'Even though Tabeth is a maiden, she is not yet fully grown. It would be better to wait a while longer.'

'But I love her Amai, and besides I miss my brothers. It would be nice to have a companion; someone to share my rondavel, to talk to at night.'

Amai smiled at her youngest child. 'Chikomo, it all depends on Tabeth's father, and your brothers who will provide the *lobola* for you from the family herd. You should talk to them. Mahachi is expected soon, he is coming to collect Salomé now that her work in the fields is finished.'

'Yes, I will do that; talk to Mahachi when he comes.'

A few days later, Usai drove into the village with Mahachi as his passenger. Chikomo beamed at the sight of them. He had not lost his boyish expressions of delight, but he no longer launched himself at them as they climbed out of the car; he had developed a measure of manly sophistication.

'Will you both stay with me in my rondavel tonight?' he said excitedly. 'I would like your company.'

'Of course we will little brother,' said Usai.

Mahachi left his brothers talking, and walked towards

Amai and Ambuya. They both laughed with pleasure at the sight of him; a mischievous twinkle appeared in Ambuya's eyes.

Amai embraced him. 'It is good to see you, my son. Salomé has worked hard in the fields, in spite of feeling so unwell. I look forward to her return after the rains, to help with the harvest.'

'She has been unwell? What was the matter with her?' asked Mahachi, a look of concern on his face. 'Have you taken her to the *nganga*?'

'No, there was no need. Salomé is over there,' said Amai, pointing to the far side of the village. 'Go and talk to her.' Mahachi hurried away.

The people he passed smiled. '*Makorokoto!*' some said. Congratulations. He looked at them, baffled. He saw Salomé rushing towards him.

'What has happened? Amai said you have been unwell, yet everyone is smiling.'

'Of course they are. I am not unwell because I am ill; I am unwell because I am going to be a mother, Mahachi.'

The village filled with the sound of his laughter, his happiness. 'When will our child be born?'

'In the middle of the dry season.'

At the other end of the village Usai left Chikomo and joined his mother. 'Are you well, Amai? You look weary.'

'I am well enough.' She sighed. 'But even with Salomé's help, it is difficult to complete the planting in time for the main rains.'

'Let us sit down so that we can talk. I have some good news for you, Amai.'

'Has Neli decided to come?' Usai saw her face brighten.

'No Amai, she has not, but she is expecting a child, you are going to be a grandmother.'

'Soon I will have two grandchildren,' said Amai smiling. 'Salomé is also expecting a baby.' The expression on Amai's

151

face became serious. 'This news of a child may change things in your favour, Usai.'

'That is what I am hoping. I have no wish for a separation from Neli, now that she is expecting my child and I cannot return her to Khumalo, her father, claiming that she is barren and therefore an unsatisfactory wife. Before I leave here I am going to ask Little Father to speak to the senior elder and plead for me. Perhaps my child will make a difference.'

'Go to Little Father now, Usai. The elders will take some time to discuss the matter and come to a decision. Let us hope they find a solution; I have no wish to ban my own son from his birthplace.'

Usai and Little Father spent most of the day together, talking in low voices that could not be overheard. The family meal that night was a pleasant gathering.

'I hear that I am to have two great-grandchildren,' said Ambuya, as she spooned some food onto her plate. 'I hope the spirits do not come for me before the infants are born.'

Her two eldest grandsons looked at her. She was very old and wrinkled now. They had both noticed that she walked more slowly and used a stick but otherwise she seemed in good health.

'I hope you will still be here, Ambuya,' said Mahachi, distressed by her words. 'I would be very sad indeed if you did not hold my first-born in your arms.'

'I too,' said Usai, 'but I do not think you will be leaving us yet, Ambuya. I notice that you have not lost your appetite. So far you have eaten two platefuls of the food that Mahachi brought from the hotel and now you are filling a third.'

Ambuya chuckled.

Later, in Chikomo's rondavel, the three brothers talked far into the night.

'I want to marry Tabeth,' announced Chikomo. 'Both of

you will soon have children; I am lagging behind.' Mahachi and Usai stifled their laughter.

'How will you provide for Tabeth and the children you will have, Chikomo?' asked Mahachi.

'I am planning to learn more carpentry skills; my work will be sent to the Craft Village to be sold. Tabeth is learning to sew and crochet so that she can do the same.'

Mahachi put his arm round Chikomo's shoulders. 'I am proud of you,' he said.

'You are doing well little brother but there is no need for you to marry yet,' said Usai. 'I think it would be best if you ask Little Father to begin the negotiations after our children are born. You could hold the marriage ceremony at the end of next year.'

'And remember Chikomo, when the time comes if other offers are made for Tabeth we will offer more,' said Mahachi. 'There are plenty of goats in the family herd.'

'Supposing someone approaches Tabeth's father before your children are born,' said Chikomo, anxiously.

'If you are troubled, you could ask Little Father to speak for you now and request a long period of betrothal,' said Usai.

Chikomo sat thinking, considering his brothers' words. 'Yes, that is what I will do. Then nobody can take Tabeth from me.'

The following morning, after his brothers and Salomé had departed, Chikomo walked across the village to where Little Father was sitting. 'Little Father I would like to speak to you.'

'What is it, Chikomo?'

'I want to marry Tabeth. I have spoken to Amai who says I should wait a while until Tabeth is fully grown.'

Little Father nodded.

'Usai and Mahachi think I should wait until the end of next year, after their children are born,' Chikomo continued.

'Chikomo, you are still young. Do you expect to spend the rest of your life in the village, or might you wish to follow your brothers? You should consider these things first.'

'I have no interest in the town. I know that I belong here.'

Little Father smiled. 'It is good to know that not all our young people are being enticed away from the village.'

'I would like Tabeth's father to know my intentions. Usai suggests that I request a long betrothal. Will you speak to Tabeth's father for me, Little Father?

'Of course, if that is what you wish.'

Later that day Tabeth's father, Moyo, asked to speak to Chikomo.

'It has not gone unnoticed, Chikomo, that you are growing into a fine young man and that my daughter follows you around at every opportunity. Little Father tells me that you have requested a long betrothal to Tabeth. I would have no objections to such an arrangement but I would like to speak to Usai first. I require some assurances. Next time he visits the village I wish to talk to him.'

When Usai reached town he drove Mahachi and Salomé to their cottage. The mopane trees along the Close were now in full leaf, providing a dark green canopy of shade for the cottages. The hibiscus hedge surrounding number three was thick with new growth and large red flowers.

Walking through the open gate, Salomé noticed that where there had been bare earth, now many plants were growing.

'How different the front garden looks, Mahachi. You have been busy while I was away. What is the name of those plants?' she asked, pointing to the small palm-like evergreens.

'They are cycads,' said Mahachi, 'and the shrubs with clusters of yellow flowers are yellow elders. Come and see what I have put in the back garden.'

The previously uncultivated area behind the cottage was now planted with rows of mealies and pumpkins.

'Mahachi, you have started a vegetable garden,' Salomé said, delighted.

'Yes and soon I shall bring other seedlings for you to plant, as well as the busy lizzies you are planning to grow along the drive.'

They smiled at each other.

'I was looking forward to visiting my family and friends at the village and yet after a few days I longed to be back here at our home.'

'When I came to the cottage it was quiet; you were not here singing as you worked at one of your tasks. I had difficulty sleeping without you beside me.'

'You said you would not miss me at all; that you planned to spend your spare time at the beer hall.'

'I changed my mind.'

Mahachi was content. The upheaval of moving into town, the emotional turmoil of his brief relationship with Janacen, followed by his deep concern that he might have caught a disease, were now past. With Salomé he felt safe. He had a routine and happy life with no unwelcome surprises.

That night in bed he ran his hand gently over Salomé's body, lingering at the place where his tiny unborn infant was growing, feeding and protected. He held her in his arms. 'I love you,' he said.

23

'Mahachi, when will I see you again?' asked Salomé.

'I will come home as often as I can but Christmas and New Year are one of our busiest times at the hotel, we have many extra duties to do. They pay me more money, so you will be able to buy the things you need for our baby.'

'Hmm. When you are less busy we could go to the city to do some shopping.'

'It would be unwise to travel so far while you are pregnant. The journey is long and uncomfortable. I will send for a catalogue from the wholesaler where I bought our furniture. In the evenings, you could spend time deciding what you are going to order.'

'I can have anything I like?' she asked eagerly.

'I would prefer you not to spend all my money. Choose only the items you will need for our child.'

'But soon my dresses will no longer fit me. Do you expect me to walk through the town with safety pins holding the front of my clothes together?'

Mahachi laughed but did not answer. There was something more important he wanted to discuss with her.

'I have heard that many women in town visit modern doctors when they are expecting a child.'

'I do not use modern medicine. I will go to the *nganga* in the Craft Village if I need any remedies.'

'I would not like the other women in the Close to think badly of you; to believe that your husband cannot

156

afford the best medical care for his wife and child.'

Salomé stared at him. 'Is that what they would think?'

'They might.'

She did not speak for a while. 'Perhaps the next time I go into town I will visit the surgery,' she said eventually, 'just to take a look.'

Mahachi loved the hustle and bustle of the Christmas season. He enjoyed watching the chefs prepare the Christmas fare, mixing and cooking the puddings and pies which filled the kitchen with mouthwatering aromas; seeing the turkeys and hams being hung in the cold storage room.

The walls of the hotel lounge were decorated with lines of Christmas cards hanging on red ribbons; greetings from past tourists. Sometimes, when Mahachi was free, he studied the pictures on the cards bearing symbols of a religion and culture to which he did not belong. It fascinated him to see the unfamiliar scenes; men on camels riding across a desert, a single bright star illuminating the sky; a man with a long white beard wearing a comical red outfit, on his back a sack full of brightly wrapped parcels; tall spiky trees decorated with shiny coloured balls and tiny twinkling lights. Mahachi knew something of Christianity because some members of staff were Christians but he neither gave nor received cards.

It came as a surprise when Everjoy, at reception, handed him an envelope. He looked at the stylish handwriting and the colourful festive stamps, with a round symbol stamped on each of them. He slid his finger along the flap and pulled out a Christmas card. It was a snowy scene, with a blanket of white on the ground and mountains in the background. He opened the card. It was signed by Janacen. He went to his room and shut the door.

Once inside he spread the contents of the envelope on the bed. In addition to the card there was a single sheet of folded paper, it was a brief letter. Inside the letter was a photograph.

He recognised her smiling face immediately. She had the same long fair hair and startling blue eyes. Her once golden skin was now pale. Studying the picture, he recalled the misery he had endured after her departure. On her lap was a tiny child, the antithesis of Janacen in appearance. The child's curly hair was a rich brown colour, much darker than its skin; small dark eyes, fringed with thick lashes, stared out of a round face.

Mahachi read the letter.

Dear Mahachi,
I have thought of you often since I returned to my own country. The picture on the card is a scene I once described to you. Do you remember? The child on my lap is my daughter. I have named her Ebony to remind me of her father's dark beauty. I thought you would like to see a picture of her. I do not intend to return to Africa but perhaps one day Ebony will want to travel there, to find her father. With happy memories of the time we shared together,
Affectionately, Janacen

Bewildered, Mahachi stood holding the letter for some time before putting the envelope and its contents at the back of his wardrobe.

In the hotel kitchen Mahachi and Mpofu were busily working together. Mahachi was dipping fillets of fish into beaten egg and breadcrumbs, before frying them in hot oil. Mpofu was garnishing the fish mornay he had made with freshly picked sprigs of parsley.

'When we have some free time I need to talk to you privately, Mpofu.'

Mpofu looked up from what he was doing. 'Does this have anything to do with your last problem?'

'Yes.'

'We have no time for long talks at present but I can spare you a few minutes after lunch tomorrow. I will come to your room.'

Sitting on Mahachi's bed, the following afternoon, Mpofu examined the photograph and read the letter.

'When did you receive these?'

'Yesterday.'

'Is it the first time that Janacen has written to you?'

'Yes. I have heard nothing from her since she left here. The letter was a surprise to me. Why has she written now?' asked Mahachi.

'She wanted to tell you about Ebony.'

'I do not understand.'

'In other cultures there are young women, I am told, who wish to have a child but do not want to marry, strange though that may seem to us. I believe that is what has happened here.'

'You think Janacen wanted a child?'

'Yes. Your child it would seem.'

Mahachi looked at the photograph again. 'My daughter,' he said. 'What should I do, Mpofu?'

'Nothing. You cannot visit your child, she is too far away and there is no address given here, so you cannot reply to the letter. I believe Janacen wants the child for herself. But she is preparing you; letting you know that in the years to come Ebony may wish to visit you.'

'What shall I tell Salomé?'

'It would be foolish to tell her anything, Salomé would be jealous. Your life together might become very unpleasant.'

'I intend to keep the picture of Ebony even though we may never meet. I will hide the photograph here in my room, at the back of the wardrobe where it will not be seen by others.'

'That would be wise.'

'How can I be sure the child is mine,' said Mahachi, as an afterthought. 'Janacen went to Kariba after she left here.'

Mpofu laughed. 'Look at the child's eyes, Mahachi.'

24

It was two weeks since Usai had last spoken to Little Father asking him to plead with the senior elder. After Neli left for work, Usai took the car and drove slowly out to the village. He was hoping the day would bring a solution to his problems.

It was nearing the end of the rainy season; the grass along the route was tall and green, and the trees were now loaded with seed pods. Large pale sausage-shaped fruits dangled from long stalks on the kigelia tree.

He wound down the window and breathed deeply; the pleasant aroma of herbivores pervaded his nostrils. He slowed the car and scanned the area. He noticed a herd of zebra moving through the dense bush. Several of them paused and turned to look at him before continuing on their way.

Further on he noticed that the nests of the golden weavers, suspended from branches above the river, were now empty. The chicks had fledged. As he caught sight of them flitting over the water he could see that their wings were still green, in contrast to the golden yellow of the adults.

There were no members of his family in sight when he drove into the village. In the distance he could see the women in the fields, harvesting fresh green mealies. He climbed out of his car and walked across to Little Father's rondavel.

'*Mangwanani* Little Father. Are you well?'

Little Father woke with a start; he had been dozing in his chair. He stood up unhurriedly, stretched his arms and yawned.

'*Mangwanani* Usai,' he said eventually. 'Neli has not accompanied you, I see.'

'No Little Father, she has not. Were you able to speak to the senior elder on my behalf?'

'Yes I was. He said he would be willing to see you. This would be a good time for you to visit him. With the women in the fields, your conversation is unlikely to be overheard.'

The senior elder sat opposite Usai on a carved wooden chair. He spoke in earnest. 'I understand that your wife Neli has refused to fulfil her duties to Amai. Is this correct?'

'Yes elder, it is.'

'This is a serious matter, Usai; you have broken your pledge to me at your marriage ceremony. It is the custom to ban you, to deny you the right to visit our village, to disinherit you from the land that belonged to your ancestors.'

'Is there no other way?'

The elder paused before answering. 'I have been told there is to be a child.'

'Yes elder, it is due after the rainy season.'

'To resolve your problem it would be necessary for you to bring the infant to live with Amai, at a suitable time during its first year of life. The child must remain with her and attend the village school to learn our traditions. Of course, Neli would be entitled to visit her first-born whenever she chose.'

'But she would not be welcome here.'

'That is true but no harm would come to her.' The elder looked at Usai; his gaze was long and piercing. 'If you agree to these demands you will avoid being banned. Amai will regain the respect of the villagers and your sons will retain their right to inherit the land.'

'Elder, I want my children to attend the secondary school in the town.'

'I understand. Your first-born would be returned to you at the appropriate time.'

Usai sat in silence, contemplating the grave task that lay before him, considering the effect it would have on his already crumbling marriage. *If only Neli ...* It was no use, she would never change her mind. He steeled himself.

'I thank you for your advice elder and agree to your demands. In due course, I will deliver my child into Amai's care.'

He stood up, shook the elder's hand respectfully and walked outside feeling both relief and sadness. A voice called his name. 'Usai, Usai.' It was Chikomo. 'I did not know you were coming here today. I am very pleased to see you.'

'Hello Chikomo.'

'I have spoken to Tabeth's father, as you suggested, and he has no objections to a long betrothal but he would like to speak to you. He says he needs some assurances.'

'Chikomo, I do not intend to stay here long, I came for a purpose and I have no wish to embarrass Amai. Neli is not with me. Do you understand what that means?'

'Yes Usai, I do.' Chikomo's eagerness vanished.

Usai saw the look of disappointment on his young brother's face and felt guilty. 'I do not want to be noticed Chikomo, but I am willing speak to Tabeth's father in the privacy of his rondavel. Go quickly and ask if he is prepared to see me.'

'I have heard, Usai, that your wife Neli is refusing to help Amai in the fields. Is this true?' asked Moyo, Tabeth's father.

'Yes it is.'

'Is it possible that she will change her mind?'

'No Moyo, she will not.'

'That is a pity. If Tabeth and Chikomo were to marry, my wife and daughter would be tainted by the disgrace that will fall upon your family.'

'There will be no disgrace. I have spoken to the senior elder this morning and he has shown me a way to resolve my problems.'

'Aaah. And when will that happen?'

'In due course.'

'I need some assurances before I agree to negotiate with Little Father.'

'If you speak to the senior elder I am certain he will reassure you.'

'We shall see,' said Moyo.

Usai's words were not as polite as was customary; thoughts of Neli were invading his mind, making him angry. Her wilfulness was now beginning to affect Chikomo's life and that was intolerable.

25

Usai drove through the open gate of number three Mopane Close, where Mahachi was waiting for him in the drive.

'Your message sounded serious,' said Mahachi, as he climbed into the passenger seat.

'It concerns Chikomo.'

'Has something happened to him?'

'Do you recall the conversation we had with him about his marriage to Tabeth?'

'Yes I do.'

'When I visited the village recently I spoke to Tabeth's father, Moyo. I was troubled by his reluctance to negotiate with Little Father. I am driving to the village today, to speak to Moyo again. I want you to come with me, I need your support.'

'Of course I will come. Does this have anything to do with Neli?'

'Yes it does.'

Mahachi made no comment. It was not his place to criticise the wife of his older brother. They spoke very little as they drove along Zambezi Drive.

At the village Usai and Mahachi sat facing Moyo inside his rondavel.

'I have spoken to the senior elder and he has confirmed what you said at our last meeting Usai: that a solution to your problems has been reached. I have given the matter much thought. You understand that I have my family to protect.

165

Once I see evidence that your difficulties are resolved, the negotiations can begin.'

'But that will not be for some time,' said Usai, deeply agitated.

Moyo made no comment.

'What if you were approached by another,' said Mahachi.

'Naturally I would consider the offer.'

'You know how fond Tabeth is of Chikomo; she would not wish to marry someone else.'

'I have no obligation to please my daughter, Mahachi. When has that ever been a consideration?'

'Whatever you were offered, we would be prepared to offer more. Would you at least give us that opportunity; get word to us that you have been approached?' pleaded Usai.

'Usai, you know that is not the custom,' said Moyo. 'I am not obliged to discuss the offers I receive but even if I agreed to such a thing, that is not the issue here. The issue is the disgrace.'

Mahachi went to sit with his grandmother.

'I will send word to you if I hear any news concerning an offer for Tabeth,' she said. 'Little Father and I will eavesdrop as often as we can. I have loyal friends Mahachi, who will keep me informed.'

'They might have been loyal to you once, Ambuya, but now that our family is on the point of disgrace, you can no longer guarantee their loyalty.'

Some weeks later, the scene that greeted Usai and Mahachi as they drove into the village was one of turmoil. Chikomo was pacing back and forth, shouting unintelligible words between sobs; tears streamed down his distraught face. Amai was attempting to comfort him, but each time she touched his arm he brushed her hand away.

In the centre of the village Little Father was loudly remonstrating with Moyo. Little Father's raised voice was full

166

of anger; his hands gesticulated accusingly in front of Moyo's face. Villagers had gathered around them to listen, some offering opinions of their own.

Usai and Mahachi flung open the doors of the car. Usai hurried towards Little Father while Mahachi rushed to where Chikomo was now sitting on the ground, his hands covering his face. Mahachi knelt down beside him. 'What is wrong?'

At the sound of his brother's voice, Chikomo looked up. 'You promised. You promised me that you would offer more,' he said accusingly.

'Tell me what has happened.'

'Tabeth's father has accepted an offer.'

'Whose?'

'It is a young man from the next village. He has a rich relative in the city who already contributes many goats to their people.'

Mahachi knew who that young man was; his name was Jaya, he had bid for Salomé. He stood up and walked briskly towards Usai.

'I am not obliged to discuss my negotiations with you,' Moyo was saying to Usai. 'It is my duty to support my family, to negotiate for as much as possible. I have accepted Jaya's generous offer of eighteen goats, which I will receive shortly.'

'But we would have offered more had you given us the opportunity,' said Usai, angrily.

'Under the circumstances I could not do that.'

Usai and Mahachi walked away in despair.

Across the village, Amai sat down beside Chikomo, murmuring consoling words to ease his misery. Chikomo sensed that somebody was standing behind them. He looked round. It was Ina, Tabeth's mother.

'I ... I am looking for Tabeth, I do not know where she is. Have you seen her?'

'No, she has not been here, Ina. When did you last see her?' asked Amai.

'It was just after her father told her that she was betrothed to Jaya. She ran into the rondavel, crying. I went to speak to her later but she was no longer there.'

Chikomo dried his eyes on his T-shirt. He knew exactly where Tabeth would go but he kept silent. He moved away from the two women and went inside his rondavel. There he rolled up his large blanket in readiness and waited.

At sundown many women were standing in groups discussing the day's events; men had been sent out to search for Tabeth beyond the village. As the light faded, Chikomo picked up his torch and blanket and slipped quietly away, unseen by all except one.

He made his way down to the thickly wooded area close to the Hippo Pool, to the place where he kept his dugout canoe covered by old mealie meal bags and hessian sacks, and concealed by branches and twigs. Switching on his torch Chikomo saw that the branches and coverings had been removed. He shone the light inside the canoe. Tabeth was curled in a foetal positon, she was shivering from shock.

'It's me, Tabeth,' Chikomo whispered.

She looked up. 'Chikomo, what are we going to do? I do not want to marry Jaya. I would rather drown in the great river.'

Chikomo climbed into the dugout beside her. Reaching out he pulled some of the branches back over the canoe to camouflage it. Using Chikomo's large blanket to cover themselves, the two of them lay side by side, traumatised and exhausted.

As darkness fell the men stopped searching and walked back to the village. Some of the men from Jaya's village had joined them but Tabeth had not been found.

'Let us take the car, Usai, and see if we can find Tabeth,' said Mahachi.

Usai looked at Mahachi in surprise. He was about to speak when Mahachi silenced him. 'Sssh! Drive beyond sight of the village and I will explain,' he whispered.

'Where are we going?' asked Usai, as he drove the car out of the village and parked it by the old baobab.

'I saw Chikomo leave the village. He was carrying a blanket. I believe I know where he and Tabeth are; I think they have gone to the Hippo Pool, to the dugout.'

'Why did you not say?'

'I do not intend to betray Chikomo. We will park the car close to their hiding place and keep watch throughout the night.'

'We dare not, Mahachi. It is taboo for them to spend the night together, unmarried; there would be serious consequences. They would be driven out of the village. If you know where Tabeth is, we must return her to her mother.'

'So that Tabeth is forced to marry Jaya? Chikomo would never recover from such a shock. Have you forgotten how he suffered when Pita died? I have a plan. You must trust me, Usai.'

'I cannot!'

'You must!'

Usai shook his head but said nothing further. He let off the handbrake and allowed the car to slip silently down to the Hippo Pool. He parked at the very edge of the woods. 'Where does Chikomo keep the canoe?'

Mahachi pointed. 'In among those trees.'

Taking his torch out of the glove compartment, Usai shone it through the vegetation.

'There,' said Mahachi, catching sight of the canoe, 'the coverings have been disturbed. We will take it in turns to keep watch.'

'I will take the first watch,' said Usai, turning off his torch. 'I doubt that I will be able to sleep.'

While Mahachi dozed, Usai sat worrying. He took no pleasure watching the hippos leave the river to graze on the lush grass along its bank, the moonlight outlining their rotund bodies. Deep in thought, he paid no attention to the distant sound of the mighty river, as it sped towards The Falls.

Mahachi's eyes strayed upstream towards the east. The sky was beginning to lighten. He shook Usai. 'It is time,' he said. They made their way through the trees. When they reached the canoe they removed the branches which covered it and looked down at the innocent faces of the sleeping pair.

'Chikomo,' said Usai. 'Chikomo,' he said more loudly. Chikomo's eyes opened, startled he sat up. 'Bring Tabeth and come with us.'

When the four of them were seated in the car Mahachi turned round to face Chikomo and Tabeth. 'This is what we are going to do,' he said.

Several women including Amai were already at the cooking area making tea when Tabeth walked into the village. The women called out her name.

'Tabeth.'

Hearing her daughter's name, Ina rushed out of her rondavel, took Tabeth into her arms and led her away.

Shortly afterwards, Usai drove his car into the village and parked it in the usual place. The three brothers climbed out and went into Chikomo's rondavel. Amai brought them mugs of hot tea. Usai raised his hand to silence her as he saw the look in her eyes. 'Ask no questions Amai, it is best if you do not know.'

Villagers gathered together in groups to talk. From time to time one of them pointed a finger at Ina's rondavel, another at Chikomo's.

It was about mid-morning that Moyo received a visitation. Jaya's relatives had come to call. Moyo greeted them warmly and invited them into his rondavel; his family brought stools for them to sit on and refreshments to drink. A group of people, including Ambuya and Little Father, stood nearby in the hope of hearing a random word. Mahachi joined them.

'I understand that Tabeth has returned safely,' said Jaya's father.

'That is so,' said Moyo.

'I was told that she spent the entire night away from the village unaccompanied, and that shortly after her return some young men drove into the village. They too had been absent throughout the night. I was informed that one of them had hoped to marry her.'

'That is also correct. However, my wife assures me that Tabeth has come to no harm; she is still a maiden.'

'That may be true Moyo, but it is a great embarrassment to our family who have offered you a generous *lobola* for her. Such behaviour is not to our liking. Jaya is not sure that he wishes to marry such a wayward young woman.'

'But we have negotiated and my wife has given her assurances.'

'Even if Jaya is still prepared to marry Tabeth, our family would no longer be willing to pay such a large *lobola*. We would be prepared to offer only four goats.'

'Four goats,' whispered one of the eavesdroppers outside. The words were circulated.

'Four goats are an insult to my family. I could never accept such an offer.'

Jaya's relatives stood up and went outside.

'Wait, can we not ...'

They turned their backs on Moyo, walked past the eavesdroppers and out of the village.

Mahachi smiled.

171

26

Usai arrived home late on Wednesday evening. He found Neli in the bedroom, preparing for bed. He stood in the doorway watching her. She was nearing the end of her pregnancy. He walked across the room and gently ran his hand over the swollen breasts that would nourish his offspring. He caressed the smooth contour of the belly that was nurturing his child, keeping it warm and safe. Her pregnant form rekindled a feeling of affection within him. Impulsively, he led her to the bed and for the first time in many months, he made love to her. Her low murmurs became cries of pleasure. Afterwards, she buried her face in the crook of his neck and sobbed with relief.

Their relationship changed. They no longer quarrelled. They were pleasant to each other during the short periods they spent together.

'I think you should ask your mother to stay here with you, when your maternity leave begins. You will need someone to help you while I am away in the bush.' Besides Neli's wellbeing, Usai was considering his own future. It would be important to deliver a healthy child into Amai's safekeeping, when the time came.

Some weeks later, Usai arrived home in a cheerful mood. It had been an enjoyable week for him at Kudu Camp. Now that the rainy season was over, the thick mud on the dirt tracks had dried out and the routes were passable again. He was able to extend his tours into the remoter, wilder areas of the game reserve.

He opened the front door and walked into the chalet. He heard Neli groaning.

'Neli?' he called.

'We are in the bedroom.'

He found her sitting on the bed. Tandai, her mother, was massaging Neli's lower back. A holdall stood on the floor.

'It is time,' said Tandai.

The local hospital was a long, single-storied building, with an added wing at either end. It was grey in colour with a green, tiled roof. Usai parked his car in the car park and walked round to the other side of the vehicle, to assist Neli. Her cumbersome body made it difficult for her to struggle out of the small passenger seat. Tandai climbed out of the back carrying the holdall, and the three of them walked slowly towards the west wing, the maternity hospital. Inside, Neli uttered a loud groan.

'Sit on this bench my daughter. I have some *muti* here from the *nganga*. It will ease your pain.'

'No mother, I do not use the old remedies. I will wait for the modern doctor.'

Usai looked up and down the corridor. There was nobody to be seen. He called out. 'Can somebody help me? My wife ...'

A midwife appeared from one of the rooms along the passageway and walked unhurriedly towards them. She wore a spotless white uniform and her short blonde hair was covered by a white starched cap. When she reached them, Usai noticed that the badge she was wearing bore the name Sister van Rensburg.

Neli's groans turned to shouts of anguish; her face contorted with pain.

'What a lot of fuss. Is this your first baby?' the sister asked, unsympathetically.

'Yes sister,' Neli whimpered, still in distress.

'And your name?'

'Neli.'

The sister glanced at Usai. 'There's no need for you to wait, come back later,' she said, dismissively.

'I intend to help my wife to walk to the ward and I will leave when she is comfortable.'

They stared at each other. The sister finally turned away. 'Come, follow me,' she said, abruptly.

Supporting Neli by the arm, Usai helped her walk with difficulty along the corridor and into the ward. Tandai picked up the holdall and followed, a smile on her lips.

At the chalet Usai wandered into the nursery. A large cot stood on a colourful mat in the centre of the room. A small wardrobe was standing in the corner. He opened the doors and examined the items of tiny clothing that were hanging on a rail. He pulled open a drawer lower down and touched the miniature vests, little bigger than his hand. He closed the wardrobe doors and looked around. The unoccupied room was silent, waiting.

In the sitting room Usai sat on the sofa. He contemplated the coming infant, and the task that lay before him. Chikomo and Tabeth were now betrothed and their marriage planned for the latter part of the year. Chikomo's marriage would be a good time for him to leave the child with Amai. He relaxed, dozed and drifted into sleep.

He awoke with a start. A dim light was beginning to filter in through the windows. It was dawn.

He found Neli in the small ward where he had left her. She was holding his child in her arms, smiling down at it. The infant was already suckling greedily at her breast. He sat on the bed and looked down at the child who would redeem his position in the village.

'We have a son.'

'He is a fine boy, Neli.' He touched his son's cheek gently

and smiled. 'He looks large and strong, we shall call him Shumba.'

The following day Usai walked into the Registry Office, the small brick building with the red roof where he and Neli had held their civil ceremony. He approached the counter.

'Can I help you?' asked a young man.

'I would like to register my son; his name is to be Shumba.' Half an hour later Usai left the office with a birth certificate.

Neli brought Shumba home a few days later. The previously silent nursery was suddenly full of life.

27

Mahachi opened the front gate and strolled towards his cottage. The driveway was now vibrant with banks of busy lizzies, in vivid shades of pink, red and magenta. He found Salomé in the back garden. She was eating a mealie cob. He noticed that the weight and size of their unborn child had altered her posture, forcing her to lean backwards. She was wearing a white blouse and a sarong-style skirt that reached her ankles.

With difficulty, Salomé had been harvesting cucurbits, large orange-skinned pumpkins, small dark green gem-squash and pear-shaped butternuts. A colourful mound was stacked outside the kitchen door.

'You have done well, Salomé. It is a fine crop. Let me help you to carry them inside,' said Mahachi. 'We can store them in one of the kitchen cupboards.'

'Do not place them too high; I am having difficulty reaching the upper shelves now.'

They walked back and forth into the kitchen; Mahachi walking briskly and Salomé waddling slowly. When their task was complete they sat down at the kitchen table.

'I think my mother should come for a visit,' said Salomé. 'My time is close and I need someone here with me when you are away.'

'Yes, of course.' Mahachi reminisced. 'I promised your father long ago that I would invite your mother to stay with us. I said you would take her shopping at the Craft Village. I was told that she liked trinkets.'

'I want my mother here with me when the baby comes, not in the town choosing necklaces and bracelets.'

Mahachi laughed. 'I will fetch her tomorrow.'

Salomé went outside to greet her mother, Nettie, who had come with a great deal of luggage, including cardboard boxes. Mahachi helped Nettie to carry her belongings into the spare bedroom. The previously austere room was now brightly decorated with soft furnishings; Salomé had made them with fabric that Mahachi had purchased in the city. Delicately patterned curtains in shades of green hung at the windows and matching bedspreads covered the two single beds.

'The curtains and bedspreads are very beautiful. I can see that you have been busy, my daughter.' Nettie sat on one of the beds and bounced up and down. 'Eeee,' she exclaimed, 'a very soft bed.'

'Mahachi and I will leave you to unpack, mother. I will make us some tea and take it into the living room. You can join us when you are ready.'

Some time later Nettie emerged from the spare bedroom with two cardboard boxes which she put on the floor by the sofa. She sat down. Salomé knelt on the floor to serve her mother tea, as was the custom.

'What have you there, mother-in-law?' asked Mahachi, pointing to the boxes.

'They are gifts from me and my family to your first-born.'

From the boxes she took out carefully folded pieces of newspaper, each in the shape of a parcel. She opened each package slowly. Mahachi and Salomé watched. Within each sheet of paper was a delicate item for an infant.

'These are to keep the child's head warm during the cold times to come,' said Nettie, displaying a collection of tiny woollen hats knitted in intricate patterns, each with a pompom on the crown. She unfolded garment after garment

177

of skilfully made baby clothes. 'This took me a long time to make.' Proudly she held up a thick white shawl, crocheted in wool with fringes hanging from the lower edges.

Salomé and Mahachi were delighted. They cupped their hands and clapped, in a customary gesture of thanks.

'Mother, let us put the clothes away until they are needed. Come, I will show you where they will be kept.'

Mahachi watched them from the door of the nursery as they folded each article and laid it in a drawer at the bottom of one of the wardrobes. He listened to mother and daughter engage in womanly chatter and gossip. For a moment he felt left out.

'I must go back to work now, Salomé,' he said.

Salomé walked with him to the front door. 'Your mother has been very generous; perhaps you will change your mind about taking her to the Craft Village.'

Just after dawn Mahachi walked out of his bedroom at the hotel and went down to the kitchen. Dressed in his cotton uniform and a thick sweater, he drank a mugful of the hot sweet tea provided, warming his hands on the enamel mug as he did so.

Being the middle of the dry season the weather was now at its coolest. The early mornings were chilly. Outdoors, people were walking to work wearing heavy sweaters and woollen hats. These would be dispensed with as the day progressed and the sun warmed the air.

In the hotel kitchen warm clothes were quickly discarded, when the ovens heated the room. Mahachi took off his sweater and started work.

'Isn't your baby due soon, Mahachi?' asked Mpofu.

'Yes it is. Mother-in-law is staying with us, to help Salomé and take her to the hospital if I am working.'

During the mid-afternoon break, when members of the kitchen staff were eating a meal in their dining room,

Everjoy, from reception, came into the room. She handed Mahachi a note and smiled at him.

Mahachi read the note aloud.

The maternity hospital called; your wife has just gone into labour. She requests you visit her this evening.

The staff laughed and cheered. Some of the gambling men decided to bet on whether the child would be a boy or a girl.

'Take Salomé some flowers,' said Mpofu quietly.

'Why does she need flowers? We have plenty in the garden.'

'It is a gesture Mahachi; you give them to people on special occasions.'

'Oh.'

'Ask the hotel gardener for some.'

When the evening meal at the hotel was finished and Mahachi's work for the day complete, he slipped on his sweater and walked the short distance to the hospital, carrying a bouquet of flowers; palest pink with a delicate perfume, lemon yellow and bright orange. He entered the west wing, the maternity hospital.

'Can I help you?' asked a passing midwife.

'My wife is in here. Her name is Salomé.'

'Ah yes. She is in the third ward to the left.' She smiled. 'Congratulations.'

Salomé was sitting up in bed smiling at the bundle she was holding in her arms. Mother-in-law was gossiping with a mature mother in the next bed, showing her the trinkets she was now wearing round her wrists and neck.

Mahachi approached Salomé's bed. 'These are for you,' he said, handing her the flowers.

'We have a daughter,' she said excitedly.

Peering eagerly into the thick shawl, Mahachi looked at

179

the tiny new person who would make them a family. He smiled, delighted.

'What is the name of these flowers?' asked Salomé. 'They are very pretty.'

'They are called lilies.'

'I think our daughter will be very pretty like these flowers; I would like to call her Lili.'

'Lili. Hmm. Lili is not an African name.'

'Does it matter?'

'I think our families will expect her to have an African name.'

'Perhaps we could add another name.'

Mahachi sat thinking for a while. 'Yes we could do that. We could call her mopane as well, after the trees that surround her home.'

A few days later, Mahachi walked to the small brick building with the red roof, to register his daughter Lilimopane.

28

During his work on the new rondavel, Chikomo had developed a keen interest in carpentry. He spent many hours pestering the most skilled carpenters in the village, persuading them to pass their knowledge on to him. He started creating decorative face masks, intricately carved with his own designs. Later he became more ambitious, making stools and small tables. His work was sold at the Craft Village in town.

He was sitting with Tabeth one day, watching as she embroidered a length of old hessian sacking. He marvelled that she could transform a piece of coarse material into a thing of beauty. She was using woollen yarn for her stitching, in bright shades of orange, red and yellow. With a large tapestry needle she was skilfully forming a zigzag pattern, using the colours alternately.

'What is the name of that stitching, Tabeth?'

'It is called Florentine.'

'It is very attractive. What is it used for?'

'I was told that in the city it is used to make covers for stools and chairs. Here in the village we use it to make cushion covers.'

'I would like to make two chairs, one for each of us. Do you think you could make some attractive cushions for the seats?'

'I could try. What colours would you like?'

'I am very fond of green, the colour of the bush after the rains.'

They worked together in their spare time; Chikomo

181

carefully shaping and smoothing the wood for his chairs, Tabeth working on her pieces of hessian, creating an impressive design in hues of green. Finally she sewed the pieces together and stuffed them with kapok, making them into squab cushions which could be tied securely on to Chikomo's chairs.

After several weeks their work was complete. The chairs, with their soft comfortable seats, were greatly admired.

'They will fetch a good price if you sell them at the Craft Village, Chikomo,' said Little Father.

'These are not for sale, Little Father. They are for my rondavel.'

Later, Tabeth and Chikomo sat in a quiet corner of the village discussing the success of their work.

'Little Father is right. We could make chairs with seat-cushions and sell them in town. If I improve my skills I could make other furniture as well.'

'I could design new patterns for the cushions.' Tabeth laughed excitedly. 'We could use the money to raise a fine family.'

'Yes, and when they are old enough we could teach them our skills,' said Chikomo, infected by her enthusiasm. 'You could show our daughters how to do beautiful sewing ...'

'... and you could teach our sons to do carpentry.'

'You are forgetting that I am a fisherman, Tabeth. I must teach them to fish first.'

'Of course, Chikomo. Perhaps you will have time to show them how to play football like you did ...' She stopped, suddenly aware of what she was saying.

Both of them became silent.

'I still miss, Pita.'

It had been a while since Chikomo had visited the football field at the end of the village. Boys still used it to practise dribbling and scoring goals but Chikomo was no longer involved.

This afternoon the field was empty. Chikomo walked the length of it. He crossed the dirt road and stood in front of the fence, the cordon sanitaire, which stood guarding its grisly, buried secrets. The tall grass and shrubbery were unchanged. Birds were singing melodiously in the surrounding trees. Chikomo picked up a stick and idly created patterns in the sand on the dirt road.

'Pita, are you still happy in your spirit home? Tabeth misses you.' He looked up, all was quiet and still, no Heuglin's robin came to sit on the fence as before.

'Tabeth and I are to be married. I wish you could find a way to return, then you could come and live with us.'

A light breeze rustled the leaves on the trees. It moved towards the dirt road, forming a small whirlwind which danced round Chikomo's legs several times, before moving into the tall grass and down to the river. *Was it a sign*, he thought.

From the centre of the village, Amai watched anxiously.

Later, when they were alone together, she spoke to Chikomo. 'It is a while since you took the path to the minefield,' she said, searching his face for signs of the torment he once had. 'Did you have a particular reason for going there today?'

'I was thinking how pleased Tabeth would be if Pita could find a way back from his spirit home. Then he could live with us when we are married.'

'Those who pass into the spirit world do not return, Chikomo. They are lost to us until we join them. We know Pita is happy, you and I, we saw the robin. You must be content.'

'I know Amai, but Tabeth still misses him and I am sad that he will not be here for our marriage.'

29

Shumba was six weeks old when Usai decided to take him to the village for the first of his weekly visits. He wanted to be certain that when the time came to leave his son in Amai's care, the child would be surrounded by familiar people whom he trusted.

'Take these with you Usai,' said Neli, 'they are bottle feeds made from my own expressed milk.'

Knowing that Amai would find a lactating woman who would be able to feed Shumba, he took the bottles without comment.

Usai set off with Shumba on the back seat of the car, in a carrycot. When he reached the village he parked his car in the usual place and climbed out. His family came to welcome him.

'I have brought a visitor,' he said to Amai.

Amai looked around. 'Where is the visitor,' she asked, baffled.

'In the car.'

Amai walked over to the vehicle and looked in through the windows. She clapped her hands with joy. Opening the car door, she lifted Shumba out of his carrycot. The family gathered round to catch a glimpse of the infant; the first of a new generation.

Nearby, the senior elder stopped to watch the scene. He nodded, satisfied.

The following day at the chalet, Neli had just breast-fed

Shumba and was slowly pacing the floor, holding the child against her shoulder. Usai was standing in the doorway of the nursery.

'Chikomo's marriage is planned for the end of the dry season, before the planting rains in November. You will be expected to attend.'

'I will not be welcome at the village; people will be rude and unpleasant to me. It will be humiliating.'

'Possibly. But it will be an insult to my family, and Tabeth's, if you stayed away.'

'Besides, I must return to work when Shumba is three months old; I am not entitled to more free time. My mother has already found a young girl in the township to be Shumba's nanny.'

'I am sure the chemist will give you some unpaid leave if you ask him but it is up to you. I plan to take Shumba to the marriage even if you choose not to come.'

Usai opened his eyes and looked out of his bedroom window at the chalet. Dawn was approaching. He slipped out of bed and dressed, packed some clothes into a holdall and took it into the sitting room. On the floor were two metal trunks filled with commodities for Chikomo's marriage celebrations.

Throwing back the lid of the first trunk, Usai began to check its contents. 'Mealie meal, salt, candles ...' He did the same to the second trunk; the perishables. 'Margarine, oranges, bread ...' Crated cartons of Chibuku beer stood at the side of the trunks.

'What are you doing in there, making so much noise?'

'Checking the trunks; making sure there is everything we need.'

'I have made you a mug of tea.'

He walked into the kitchen and picked up the mug. Neli was sitting at the table with their son on her lap, spoon-

185

feeding him small amounts of mealie meal porridge, before breast-feeding him. Shumba was now six months old. Neli's expression as she attended to his needs was full of happiness and love.

Usai kissed the top of his son's head. The child looked up at him and smiled, his mouth smeared with breakfast cereal. *The chalet will be quiet without your demanding presence*, Usai thought, as he stood watching his beloved son. *I shall miss the smile of recognition that greets me when I return home from the bush each week.* His gaze turned to Neli as she began to breast-feed Shumba. *If only our life together had been different.*

'I saw a holdall in the nursery. I notice you have packed many clothes for Shumba. How long do you intend to stay at the village, Usai?'

'I am not sure. The marriage ceremony is the day after tomorrow, on Saturday. The celebrations will continue for several days.'

'When do you expect to be home?'

'About mid-week,' he said evasively.

'I cannot provide you with breast milk for so many days. I would have preferred you to take the nanny with you to look after Shumba, she knows how to prepare bottle feeds,' Neli complained.

'I have no interest in the nanny, and I have already explained that Amai will take care of him and find a woman to suckle him,' said Usai, annoyed. *The same woman who has been nourishing him since I first took him to the village*, he thought.

'I cannot bear the idea of another woman feeding my child.'

'But you have chosen not to come with us. Unless you change your mind, I have no choice.'

Neli made no further comment. They heard the front gate open and the noise of the old truck being driven slowly into the drive. The engine became silent and soon footsteps could be heard on the gravel path.

'That is Mahachi,' said Usai. They went outside to greet him.

'*Mangwanani*,' Neli said to Mahachi. With Shumba balanced on her hip, she shook his hand and waved to Salomé in the truck. Mahachi greeted her politely but coldly.

'I must go to work now,' said Neli. She kissed Shumba on the cheek and handed him to Usai. 'Take good care of him,' she said, concerned. She walked to the front gate and lingered for a moment to look back at Shumba. The two brothers watched her in silence. Finally, she waved and went on her way.

'Come let us load the truck,' said Usai.

Putting Shumba on the living room floor to play, Usai and Mahachi carried the trunks and crates of beer outside and loaded them next to Mahachi's polystyrene boxes, which were full of ingredients for the dishes he intended to cook.

'I hope Chikomo will like our gifts,' said Mahachi, pointing to some large items covered in polythene.

'I am sure Chikomo will be very pleased to have a comfortable mattress and soft blankets, to start his new life with Tabeth.'

They drove slowly to the village, in convoy. Salomé sat at the front of the truck with Lilimopane on her lap; Shumba was sleeping on the back seat of Usai's car. As they drove into the village they could see that preparations had already begun for Chikomo's marriage.

Amai was waiting.

It was the last time the three brothers would spend the night together in the rondavel where they had slept as children. As they lay on the floor they talked quietly in the darkness.

'You are Shumba's Little Father, Chikomo; promise me you will help Amai to take care of him.'

'Of course I will look after my Little Son, and Tabeth will carry him on her back when Amai is tired.'

187

'I shall miss him at the chalet.'

'Will you be able to visit him each week?' asked Chikomo.

'I intend to come every Thursday and Friday but it depends on National Parks.'

'I wonder if Shumba will be as interested in wildlife as you were when you were a boy,' commented Mahachi.

'I hope so. I look forward to a time when I can pass my love of the wild on to him.'

'When you were young, you used to sneak away to the river to watch the herds go down to drink. I remember how angry the village boys would become; you should have been helping them to herd the goats or collect firewood,' Mahachi reminisced.

'Yes,' laughed Chikomo, 'and I remember the time Baba bought you a pair of very old binoculars. You did not know how to use them at first.'

'And later you would walk up and down the dirt road, using the binoculars to search the sky for fish eagles or scan the treetops for baboons. You bumped into a tree more than once,' said Mahachi.

Usai laughed. 'There was a time when I could not bear to be parted from those binoculars. I wore them round my neck even at night.'

It is good to hear Usai laugh, thought Mahachi. 'Chikomo and I were very sad when you left here, to start your training as a guide. We missed you.'

'Yes we did. You did not return for a long while.'

'I had no idea,' said Usai, deeply touched by the confessions of his siblings.

Chikomo changed the subject. 'When I have sons of my own, I hope that some will become fishermen and others carpenters.'

'Are you planning to have many sons?' teased Mahachi.

'It depends on Tabeth.'

'I think you will find it depends on you too,' said Usai.

188

Chikomo chuckled, glad that his brothers were discussing such manly issues with him. 'If I have enough money I would like to send some of my sons to learn carpentry, at the college in town where you learnt to be a chef, Mahachi.'

'While they are studying they can live with me at my cottage or with Usai at his chalet.'

'Yes. Our homes are your homes, Chikomo. Your sons will be welcome,' said Usai.

'One day Usai and I will send our daughters to you, so that Tabeth can teach them the skills of planting and reaping. They will need them when they marry,' continued Mahachi.

Usai said nothing.

The three of them lay in the darkness recalling their earliest childhood memories, reminiscing the days of their boyhood together in the village and discussing their hopes for the future. It was very late when they fell asleep. They lay close together, drawing comfort from each other as they had in their youth.

30

It was dusk, oil lamps were being lit. Two great bonfires stood in clearings at the entrances to the village; they would be kept burning throughout the night. In the bush beyond the dirt road, pairs of eyes could be seen in the deepening gloom; scavengers pacing back and forth, attracted to the smell of roasting meat, deterred by the scorching flames of the fires.

In the cooking area several men were standing by the spits, laughing and joking. They used sharp knives to carve slices of the tender, succulent goat's meat from the carcasses and place them on their enamel plates. Returning to the bar area they sat down to feast. In between mouthfuls, they took long gulps of Chibuku beer.

Cooking pots were simmering gently over small wood fires. Women and children were helping themselves to the food. Some were putting spoonfuls of stiff white *sadza* onto their dishes, others were dipping ladles into the thick chicken or vegetable relish. Afterwards they sat on colourful blankets to eat. Using their fingers they dipped lumps of *sadza* into the relishes.

'It is a fine celebration. There is plenty of food,' said one of the women.

'Mmm, the chicken relish is full of flavour; it must be one of Mahachi's special recipes,' remarked another.

'Yes, I like the taste of peanut butter in the sauce.'

In the centre of the village a group of musicians was

playing a lively tune, their fingers flashing on the curved metal keys of their *mbiras*. Around the musicians, people were dancing traditionally; men with men, women with women, swaying to the rhythm of the music. Children joined in, laughing merrily.

Amai and Usai were sitting together, watching the marriage celebrations. Shumba had fallen asleep against Usai's chest.

'Tabeth and Chikomo look very happy; they have been smiling for most of the day.'

'Chikomo has had much misery in his short life. It warms my heart to see my youngest son so full of happiness.' Amai looked at Usai. 'But for you, my first-born, I grieve. Even though you are now an accepted member of the village once more, Shumba will not live with you again for many years, not until he is old enough to attend the secondary school in town.'

Usai looked down at the sleeping child on his lap. He was overwhelmed with sadness, tears blurred his vision. 'I will visit him as often as I can,' he whispered. 'I do not want him to forget that I am his father.'

'He will not. You have my word. Might Neli come with you on your visits? She is entitled to see Shumba whenever she pleases.'

'I do not know, Amai. Neli refuses to come to the village. It is something she and I will have to discuss.'

'Whatever happens on your return home, my son, try to remember that although Neli has done us great harm, she has forfeited her first-born. For a woman that is very difficult to bear.'

Usai stood at the sitting-room window of the chalet and watched Neli walk up the drive to the front door.

'How were the celebrations?' she asked, as she entered the room.

191

'They were a great success. Chikomo is now a very happy man,' he said, following Neli as she walked towards the nursery.

She stood in the doorway of the silent room, her eyes focused on the empty cot. She spun round. 'Where is he?' Usai said nothing. 'You have left him with Amai,' she shouted accusingly.

'Yes.'

Neli slumped to the floor.

Usai stood watching her.

Silence.

It was some time before Neli could speak. 'While you were away, I took the bus and visited my mother. She demanded to know why I had not accompanied you and Shumba to Chikomo's marriage. I explained my reasons. I have never seen my mother so angry. She shouted at me. "Your father told you to be a good wife to Usai. I myself said it was your duty to be a good daughter-in-law to Amai and you have been neither. Your behaviour will bring disgrace on Usai's family and in time it will bring shame on ours."

'My mother told me what you might do. She showed me no sympathy. "You will not visit me again, my daughter, unless I send for you," she said.'

Neli turned to look again at the empty cot. The tears began to flow down her cheeks; she threw back her head and wailed the mournful cry of a woman who has lost her child, whose mother has rejected her. Uncontrollable sobs erupted from her anguished body.

Usai turned away.

Shaking and trembling she asked, 'When will I see Shumba again?'

'Neli, you can visit him whenever you choose; nobody will prevent you, you are his mother but he will be raised in the village.'

She sat up abruptly. 'You mean I can go and "view" him as I would a picture on a wall?'

192

'That is not what I meant,' he said angrily, walking into the sitting room.

Following him Neli demanded, 'How would I travel? There are no buses that go along Zambezi Drive to the village. And besides I cannot ...'

'There are several possibilities, if you are prepared to listen.'

Usai sat down at the end of the sofa, his arms crossed, his body tense. Neli sat at the other end. She dried her face with some tissues. Fresh tears spilled over the rim of her eyes and trickled down her cheeks, others followed. She cried quietly, rocking backwards and forwards.

Finally, exhausted, she shuddered. 'Tell me,' she said.

'You could arrange to take some leave and join me when I drive out to the village on my days off. Or I could ask Mahachi to take you with him, if he and Salomé visit the village at weekends.'

'I cannot, Usai ... I cannot face walking into the village, not now. I would be surrounded by people who hate me.'

'If you wish to see your son again, you will have to accept that you will be in the company of people who dislike you, who make you feel uncomfortable.'

Usai shook his head. He was exasperated, weary and sad. He covered his face with his hands. Memories of his dreadful parting with Shumba flashed across his mind.

'I have offended so many people. I have hurt your family and mine,' Neli said, in a quiet voice.

He turned and looked at her, surprised. It was the first time she had acknowledged the misery she had caused. 'Yes, you have harmed many people, including me, but I want no further discussions tonight.' He sighed. 'I am tired. I must return to Kudu Camp early tomorrow. I am going to bed. We will talk again when I come home.'

*　　*　　*

Usai was allocated a group of quiet, mature tourists. They were experienced travellers. Their sophisticated cameras indicated a serious interest in wildlife photography. He could not have endured a minibus full of boisterous young people, jumping with delight at the sight of every browsing pachyderm or dozing feline.

His days at the camp were relaxed and peaceful but his nights were restless. He lay in bed contemplating his life. He enjoyed working at Kudu Camp, deep in the bush that he loved so well. He looked forward to his days off, which he would now spend at the village with his beloved son, but it was his relationship with Neli that continued to concern him. Although they slept in the same bed at the chalet, they rarely touched unless by accident.

There are young women who live and work at the camp as I do, he mused, *and some are very beautiful.* But he was not prepared to take the irrevocable step that would destroy his marriage. He needed to be certain that he and Neli had lost all feelings for each other and could never resolve the issues that lay between them.

On Wednesday evening he drove his group back to their hotel and returned home. The smell of cooking greeted him as he opened the front door. In the kitchen Neli was preparing a meal for them.

Usai took a beer from the refrigerator and drank from the bottle. 'I am going to take a bath; I am hot and dusty from the drive.'

Later, as they were eating their meal, Neli said, 'I thought about Shumba constantly while you were away. I long to see him but I have no friends or support at the village, I dread the idea of going there. Is it possible for me to meet Amai elsewhere?'

'What do you mean?'

'Would she bring Shumba here?'

'You do not seem to understand, Neli, you are not in a

194

position to bargain. Shumba lives in the village now, with Amai. We must visit him there. You should ask the chemist for some leave, then we can visit our son together. That way you need not fear a lack of support.'

'But I want to see him every week.'

'That is not possible.'

Neli made no further reference to Shumba. During the weeks that followed Usai waited for her to announce that she had arranged some leave, but when they were together she said very little. There were long periods of silence between them.

Usai took a stroll around the garden one evening. Absently he looked at the vegetables that were growing fast, now that the rains had begun. He noticed a bicycle propped against the shed and assumed it belonged to the gardener. He was pondering Neli's current lack of communication. *I wonder if she is unwell,* he thought.

Later, he spoke to her. 'You have been very quiet recently, Neli. Are you ill? Perhaps you should make an appointment to see Dr Meyer.'

A choking sound came from her throat. 'I do not need a doctor. I am pining for my son; I miss him.'

Chikomo was working outside his rondavel, painstakingly shaping the wood for his latest chair. Tabeth was busily creating a new design for the seat cushion. They worked quietly together, occasionally smiling at each another; a secret smile, a confidence shared.

Shumba was lying on a blanket beside them. He was resting after his midday feed. The woman who breast-fed him during the day had an abundance of milk. Amai continued to give him mealie meal porridge for breakfast, as Neli had done, and also a small amount of finely mashed *sadza* and relish in the evening.

He started to cry. Tabeth stopped her work and picked him

up. Using a large towel she tied him securely onto her back. The close contact with Tabeth's body comforted him and he soon became drowsy.

Tabeth glanced at the area of bush beyond the village, her eyes moved towards the tall tree. She walked to the edge of the bush for a closer view. 'Chikomo, will you come and look?'

'What is it?' he asked, standing beside her.

'Over there,' she said, pointing. 'Can you see a woman standing by the *mdondo* tree?'

Chikomo shaded his eyes. 'Yes, I can see her. What troubles you?'

'I have seen her there before. She stands for hours watching the village. Then she disappears into the bush. Who is she?'

'I cannot see her clearly. I will fetch Amai, perhaps she knows.'

Amai stood next to Tabeth scrutinising the figure, a tall young woman with a scarf wrapped round her head, her dress old and shapeless. 'Does she always stand by the tree, Tabeth?'

'Sometimes she comes closer but she stays in the shadows.'

'How often have you seen her?'

'This is the third time.'

'Tabeth, I can see that Shumba is asleep, take him to your rondavel now. Chikomo and I will try to talk to the woman.' As Tabeth walked away, Amai whispered to Chikomo, 'I think it is Neli.'

'But why is she behaving so strangely?'

'Perhaps she is too ashamed to enter the village, or maybe she is frightened. Her actions have made her very unpopular with the women.'

'What should we do, Amai?'

'She must be approached cautiously and encouraged with kind words.'

'I will help you.'

They walked slowly towards the woman. 'Neli,' Amai called, 'you have come to visit your son at last.' The woman turned to leave. 'Do not go; you have not yet seen Shumba.' The woman hesitated and stood looking at them.

'You are welcome, Neli,' called Chikomo. 'Shumba is with Tabeth in the rondavel, come and see how fine he looks.' He and Amai stopped and waited.

Hesitantly, the woman walked towards them. Her face was now visible in the sunlight and Chikomo and Amai could see that it was indeed, Neli. Her dress was torn, her arms and legs scratched from the thorny shrubs in the bush. When she reached them, Amai took her by the arm and led her to Tabeth's rondavel.

Women who had been watching the scene turned away as Neli passed; no vindictive comments were uttered. They pitied her now.

Seeing Shumba on the floor of the rondavel, Neli let out a loud cry which echoed around the village. She swept her sleeping son up in her arms, hugging and kissing him. Tears of joy ran down her cheeks.

Neli was sitting on the sofa reading when Usai arrived home on Wednesday evening. He sat down at the end of the sofa. 'There was a letter waiting for me at the National Parks office. It was from Amai. She says you went to the village to visit Shumba. I asked you to take leave so that we could go together. Tell me what happened.'

Neli stopped reading and put her book on the coffee table. 'I went on Sunday. I have been more than once,' she began.

'Go on.'

'Usually I stand beneath a shady tree, some distance from the village. I wear old clothes, so that I am difficult to recognise. From the tree I can observe Shumba when he is outside with the family.'

'According to the letter you went into the village. You said you dreaded the idea.'

'I know but Amai and Chikomo encouraged me.' Neli turned to look at Usai, her face alight with happiness. 'Shumba has grown so big.'

'I am puzzled, Neli. How did you get to the village? Surely you did not walk.'

'Bicycle,' she mumbled with embarrassment.

'What did you say?'

'I bought an old bicycle which I leave by the shed.'

Surprising himself as well as Neli, Usai began to giggle. He visualised his beautiful, sophisticated wife, with her shapely buttocks, sitting on the small saddle, pedalling along the dusty road, the front wheel wobbling from side to side on the uneven surface. The image filled him with mirth. He burst out laughing.

'Why are you laughing?'

'Neli, it is a long way to the village and you have never cycled before.'

'I am a very good cyclist,' she said indignantly.

'No you are not,' he laughed.

'I have been practising. I started in the garden where I could not be seen. Later, I ventured onto the road outside. It was some time before I had the confidence to cycle along Zambezi Drive. The first time I went, I came home exhausted and very sore.'

'I understand why you have done this but the road to the village is dangerous, there are lions in the area.'

'I always travel during daylight hours when they are resting.'

'You can never be sure. On a bicycle you are very vulnerable.'

'I am not going to stop seeing Shumba, now that I have found the courage to go into the village,' she said.

Usai knew that she could not be deterred. The tone of

her voice reminded him how stubborn and wilful she could be.

'I have an idea,' he said. 'When I go to Kudu Camp I use a minibus, I leave my car in the office car park. If you take driving lessons and pass your test, you could use my car on Sundays.'

'Could I Usai? I would be able to see Shumba every weekend,' she said excitedly.

'There would be conditions. I would expect you to take leave, so that I could accompany you on your first drive to the village.'

Neli was too preoccupied to respond. She was smiling to herself, visualising a happier future. 'Did you say something?' she said, returning to the present.

Usai smiled, amused. 'Never mind, it will wait.'

Usai and Neli set off just after sunrise, both eager to see their son. This was the first time Neli had driven to the village. Usai had insisted that she took a day's leave, so that he could accompany her. He needed to satisfy himself that she would be able to manage the journey unaided, when he was far away at Kudu Camp.

As they approached the old baobab they could see Chikomo fishing in the shallows.

'Stop the car Neli, we must change places. The villagers will expect to see me driving the car.'

When they drew level with Chikomo Usai pressed the horn.

Chikomo looked up and waved.

'*Mangwanani*,' shouted Usai, poking his head through the open window. 'Will you be long?'

'*Mangwanani*. I shall be here a while longer, why do you ask?'

'I have something for you.'

'Do you know that the boot of your car is open?'

'Yes I do. I shall see you later.' Usai waved and drove on.

As they entered the village Usai could see Shumba sitting on a blanket with Ambuya. Leaving Neli to unpack the car he walked across to them. Usai picked Shumba up and swung him into the air; the child laughed with pleasure. Ambuya looked on, smiling.

Neli joined them. 'Good morning, Ambuya.' She shook Ambuya's hand respectfully. 'How are you today?' she asked.

'As well as can be expected, for an old woman.'

'May I take Shumba, Usai?' Neli balanced her son on her hip and walked slowly away, chattering to him as she went, her face full of happiness.

Usai sat down on a stool beside his grandmother. 'You do not like Neli, Ambuya; I hear it in the tone of your voice.'

'I am not fond of those who refuse to uphold our traditions. Like others, I am no longer fit to work in the fields. It is for the young to take the place of the old while we look after their children. If all our young women refused to help us, we would have no food growing, no store for the dry season.' She looked at Usai, his head was bowed. 'I have often noticed that you are sad, my grandson. Neli has not been a good wife. Your sadness only lessens when you are with Shumba. You would not be asked to forfeit a second child.'

He looked at her. 'How wise you are, grandmother.'

'I see that Chikomo has returned. Go and talk to him, I believe he has some news for you. I will take a rest.'

The two brothers greeted each another warmly.

'Ambuya says you have some news, Chikomo.'

'It is Tabeth,' he grinned, 'she is expecting a child at the end of the cold season. I am going to be a father, Usai.'

'So you have finally caught up with Mahachi and me, you are no longer lagging behind.'

'I know.'

Usai smiled, remembering a time when his tiny brother had longed to be a man.

'I have brought you a gift. Come.'

Usai took Chikomo behind the car to where Neli's renovated bicycle was propped against a tree. It was now freshly painted in black, with strong new tyres, a large padded saddle and a metal bell. It gleamed in the sunlight.

'A bicycle,' said Chikomo, thrilled. 'Now I can ride down to the Hippo Pool and hang my fish on the handlebars when I return.'

He wheeled the bicycle into a clearing and began to practise, riding slowly at first around the village, then at greater speed in between the rondavels, ringing the bell. Within a short time he was out on the dirt road and had disappeared from view. The sound of the bell could be heard in the distance.

Neli was sitting on a blanket in front of Amai's rondavel. Shumba sat close by, babbling as he examined the brightly coloured toys his parents had brought him. Usai lay down on the blanket beside them, propping his head on one arm so that he could watch his son.

A large brown mottled grasshopper jumped on to the blanket. Its back legs bore sharp spikes, its face was devilish. Shumba innocently stretched out his arm, attempting to reach it. Usai swept the insect away with the back of his hand. He leaned across and kissed his son's head. As he did so, he caught the smell of a light fragrance in the air; it was Neli's perfume. He rolled onto his back and watched the gentle movement of leaves on the trees overhead. *A second child*, he thought.

At dusk, when Shumba was asleep, Usai and Neli joined the family for the evening meal. As they were eating, Usai spoke quietly to his mother. 'Neli will be coming to visit Shumba every Sunday, Amai. She has now passed her driving test and will be using my car.'

Amai looked at him, surprised. 'Do women drive cars in the town now?'

'A few women do but Neli will only be using the car to visit Shumba. She has been riding a bicycle to the village, a car will be safer. She will park the car in the woodlands near the old baobab and will walk the final distance to the village. You will suffer no further humiliation.'

Usai and Neli did not stay the night at the village. It was after dark when Usai drove them back to town. On the way they talked about Shumba.

'It is so quiet at home without him, especially when you are in the bush or visiting him at the village. There is little to occupy me now. Today, for the first time in many weeks, we were a family again.' Usai noticed the catch in her voice.

It was late when they arrived back at the chalet. In the bedroom they undressed in silence. Naked, Neli was as beautiful as ever, her dark skin still smooth and unblemished. Usai stroked her shoulder. 'Perhaps another child would fill your empty hours.' Looking into her eyes, he saw they were shining. She pressed her body against his; the sensation of her warm flesh aroused him.

'Yes,' she whispered, 'another child.'

Usai surfaced from sleep; he lay uncovered and naked. Opening his eyes he saw that it was still dark outside, the chill air from the open window heralded the approaching dawn. He pulled the cotton sheet over his body.

Closing his eyes, he journeyed back through their night of renewed intimacy, recalling with surprise Neli's lustful insatiability. Drifting in and out of sleep, he recaptured images of their intense lovemaking, the moments of gentleness, fondling and exploring until they were aroused again and again.

The sky began to lighten. Usai looked across at Neli. Her back was turned towards him, her breathing even. It was a long time since his feelings for her had been so strong. His hand caressed the rounded contours of her hips and thighs.

'No more, Usai, I am tired,' she said in a drowsy voice.

He noticed the clock on her bedside table. 'Neli,' he said softly, 'it is seven fifteen.' There was no response. 'Today is Friday, you must go to work.'

Neli turned over and groaned. 'I had forgotten.' She yawned loudly. It was some minutes before she sat up and swung her legs over the side of the bed. After a while she stood up and walked slowly to the bathroom. Usai watched her smugly. He listened to the sound of running water, relieved that he did not work on Fridays.

'What are you planning to do today?' she asked, returning to the bedroom and taking a dress out of the wardrobe.

He stretched languidly. 'After such a strenuous night, I intend to spend most of the morning in bed, resting,' he teased. 'Then I shall take a long soak in the bath.'

She sat on the bed and looked at him, her eyes sparkling mischievously. Running her fingertips along his arm she said, 'I will be home as soon as I can and in the morning I promise to wake you very early, so that you can go and collect your tourists.' She picked up her bag and was gone.

31

As the sun began to set, Chikomo continued to pace back and forth, listening to the dreadful sounds that were coming from the rondavel of Tabeth's mother, Ina. He covered his ears with his hands at each new wave of screams and cries.

Alerted by Ambuya, Amai came out of the rondavel and ushered Chikomo to the other end of the village. 'Chikomo, this is not the first time you have heard such sounds; you know it is normal for a woman in childbirth. The *nganga* has sent Tabeth some *muti* to ease her labour. He will visit her as often as necessary.'

'But Amai, these sounds seem more terrible to me than others I have heard. It is as though Tabeth is struggling with the spirits.'

'The suffering is always greatest with the first-born. Come take a little food, you have not eaten today.'

'I cannot eat until I know that Tabeth has safely delivered our child.'

'Men are usually untroubled by the affairs of women, Chikomo. Childbirth is of little concern to them. Is there something else that is worrying you?'

'Of course there is Amai. Ina has already lost one child through my fault, what if she loses another?'

Amai looked alarmed, recalling Chikomo's past problems. 'Go and rest in your rondavel for a while my son, I will bring you something to drink.' She collected his enamel mug and went to Ambuya to relate her conversation with him.

'I have some *muti*, Amai, which will calm him. It is a potion I have made that induces drowsiness and untroubled sleep. Let me put a little into his mug for you.'

'It looks fresh, Ambuya, that is good; the effect will be stronger.'

'Yes it was infused recently. I use a little myself from time to time.'

Ambuya's remark did not go unheeded but Amai was preoccupied with other matters.

She found Chikomo lying on his bed and handed him a mug of freshly brewed tea. 'When you have finished your drink try to sleep for a while. I am going to return to Ina's rondavel to help with Tabeth.'

Chikomo drank the hot sweet tea with its hidden secret. He felt himself relax, his eyelids drooped.

'Chikomo, wake up Chikomo,' a voice said. Somebody was shaking him.

'What is it?' he mumbled, struggling to wake up.

'You have a son.'

'A son?' He opened his eyes.

'He is a fine strong boy,' said Amai, excitedly.

'What about Tabeth?' he asked, sitting up.

'She is very weak, the baby was large. It will take her a while to recover.'

'I must see her.' He stood up and made his way unsteadily to Ina's rondavel. Amai followed. Chikomo did not observe the usual customs but walked in through the entrance of the candlelit rondavel and knelt down beside Tabeth.

'It is not proper for you to be here, Chikomo,' said Ina.

Chikomo paid no attention. He looked down at Tabeth's face. She was sleeping, her breathing shallow. Tiny droplets of moisture covered her skin and a slight greyness was evident round her mouth. He took one of her hands between his and whispered, 'You are not going to leave me are you Tabeth? I cannot manage without you.' There was no

205

reply. He held her hand tightly. 'I shall stay here until you wake.'

'Would you like to see your son, Chikomo?' whispered Amai.

He looked at her blankly. His concern for Tabeth was so great he had given no thought to his child. 'My son?'

Amai walked over to a large basket fashioned from reeds. She picked up the child inside and carried him to his father. 'Here, take him; your first-born.'

Chikomo cradled the child in his arms. Looking down at the tiny face, he saw that the resemblance was unmistakeable.

'What will you name him?'

'Pita.' He kissed the child's forehead and held him close. 'Pita, my son.'

Outside, in the early morning light, a Heuglin's robin sang melodiously.

It was several weeks before Chikomo and Tabeth resumed their life together. After the difficult birth, the time spent in her mother's care had slowly revitalised Tabeth and her health had greatly improved. She was currently convalescing, sitting on a chair outside their rondavel embroidering cushions for Ambuya's chair. As she stitched, she watched Chikomo.

He was kneeling on a blanket with Pita, his face close to his son's. 'I promise to take good care of you, Pita.' The child stared at him. 'When you are bigger, we can go fishing together.' The infant's arms and legs moved excitedly. 'I will teach you to ride my bicycle.' The baby smiled and made cooing sounds.

Amai sat down beside them. 'I see that you are becoming acquainted with your son,' she smiled.

'I love him, Amai. It is like looking into the face of the other Pita. I will take better care of my son and make sure he comes to no harm.'

'It is possible that the spirits have sent you a child in the other's image, for just such a reason.'

32

Mahachi walked into the kitchen and took a bottle of Fanta out of the refrigerator. As he strolled into the living room he took long refreshing gulps. Salomé had not spoken since he arrived home. She was sitting on the sofa making a miniature blue cardigan for the child she was expecting in the rainy season.

'You are very quiet, is something wrong?' he asked, sitting down beside her.

She stopped knitting. 'I would like to hire a domestic to help me in the cottage and garden,' she announced unexpectedly.

Mahachi stared at her, surprised. 'You would? Why?'

'Most of our neighbours have one and I would not like them to think my husband cannot afford a domestic, particularly after his recent increase in salary.'

'I think you manage our home very well. The cottage is clean and comfortable, with all the soft furnishings you have made, and you have grown many vegetables in our small garden.'

'But I feel so embarrassed digging and planting. My hands and nails become dirty and it takes me so long to scrub them clean. Two of the women in the Close wear nail varnish and put lotion on their hands, to make them smooth and beautiful. The woman who lives at number five said, "When you have more children, Salomé, you will become exhausted attending to the needs of your family, as well as doing the housework and gardening. Your husband will start visiting the beer hall instead of coming home." I do not want you to spend your free time drinking beer.'

Mahachi smiled, amused. 'Salomé, the neighbours have made you dissatisfied, you should pay no attention to their gossip. After our next child is born you shall have your domestic, so that you will not "become exhausted attending to the needs of your family" and in time, you and I will pay a visit to the Family Planning Clinic in the township. I think two or three children will be enough to support and educate, on my "increase in salary".' He took her hand. 'It is late, let us go to bed.'

Soon after Pita's birth Mahachi drove to the village to congratulate Chikomo on the arrival of his first-born child. Mahachi arrived just as Ambuya was leaving the *nganga's* rondavel. She was carrying something in her hand; plants, *muti*. He asked her about the *muti* but she was evasive.

'Do not concern yourself with my small troubles, my grandson, they come with old age.'

Mahachi wondered what 'small troubles' she was referring to. He talked to Amai.

'She has been taking a potion which she infuses herself, but it is not for us to question her reasons.'

When he returned home, Mahachi spoke to Salomé. 'I am going to take some leave so that we can spend a few days at the village. I am concerned about Ambuya, I think she is ill. We will go on Thursday when Usai is visiting Shumba.'

On Wednesday evening Mahachi brought home a large polystyrene box which he took into the kitchen; it was full of food he was taking to Amai.

The next morning he set off early with Salomé and Lilimopane. When they reached the village, Mahachi parked the old truck behind Usai's car. He lifted Lilimopane off her mother's lap and stood her on the ground. She made her way unsteadily towards Shumba who was sitting on a blanket. Reaching it, she sat down beside him and began to examine one of his toys. Ambuya looked on as the two children sat happily, babbling and playing together.

'I am going to take the food to Amai, Salomé. She is with Usai and Chikomo at the cooking area.' He lifted the box out of the back and walked towards his mother.

Salomé climbed out of the truck and went in search of Tabeth.

'It is a pleasure to see you Mahachi, we were not expecting you today.' Seeing the polystyrene box she asked, 'What have you brought us this time, my son?'

He removed the lid and showed her the contents.

'Mm. Cold meats, rice mixed with vegetables and some sweet tarts, the food looks tasty; there is plenty for all of us. It is not often that I have all my sons and grandchildren around me, perhaps we could have our meal together at the Hippo Pool,' suggested Amai.

'You mean a picnic. I think that is a fine idea. I was planning to go to the river myself. I want to do some bird watching. We can use the vehicles to transport blankets and the food, and anyone who does not want to walk,' replied Usai.

'Will you come fishing with me, Mahachi?' asked Chikomo.

'Yes, of course I will, but first I want to talk to Ambuya.'

While the rest of the family were making preparations Mahachi walked to where Ambuya was sitting on her wooden chair, minding her great-grandchildren. He sat down beside her. 'How are you, Ambuya?' He noticed the pain in her sunken eyes.

'I am not feeling well today, Mahachi. The *nganga* has given me some strong *muti*, the pain is easing.'

'What can I do to help you?'

'Nothing my grandson, I am old. Aches and pains are to be expected.'

210

'Amai wants us to have a picnic by the Hippo Pool; I have brought food from the hotel. Are you well enough to join us? I could drive you there in the old truck.'

'It is many years since I looked upon the Hippo Pool. I used to go sometimes when your father was a fisherman. I would carry you on my back and we would sit quietly, watching him fish.'

Mahachi remembered. He recalled the smells that had wafted from her garments: wood smoke and green soap.

'I will come to the Hippo Pool, Mahachi, but I will need my chair with me.'

He drove very slowly along the dirt road, with Ambuya sitting beside him. He noticed that every jolt of the truck made her wince. He parked the vehicle in the clearing, close to the woods where Chikomo kept his dugout canoe.

'Where would you like me to put your chair?'

'There,' she pointed, 'close to that tree.'

'Your chair looks smart, with its new red cushions.'

'Tabeth made them for me. The seat is now very comfortable and I can rest my back on the other cushion.' Once settled, Ambuya said, 'I shall sit here and watch you all, and maybe sleep a little.'

She gazed at the river for a while, watching the hippos submerge and surface in the deep water by the long island. *Now that I have held Chikomo's first-born in my arms, I am content,* she thought. Her attention was attracted to the sound of laughter.

Amai had arranged several blankets on the ground. Pita was lying on his back beside his mother, gazing up at the trees. Salomé was talking to Tabeth, engaging her in womanly gossip. Periodically they would giggle.

The two inquisitive toddlers, Shumba and Lilimopane, were being closely supervised by their grandmother. No longer interested in their toys, they were eager to explore the water. They had made several attempts to toddle into the river. Each time Amai returned them to the blankets, they tried again.

Amai turned to look at Ambuya. They smiled at each other, amused. *I shall miss her so when she joins the spirits, I could not have wished for a better mother-in-law*, thought Amai. A tear rolled down her cheek. She brushed it away hastily. This was a happy family occasion.

Usai was standing at the water's edge looking through his binoculars at one of the small islands.

'What are you looking at?' called Amai.

'There is a large paradise whydah bird perched on one of the trees over there,' he gestured. 'Can you see it?'

Amai shaded her eyes. 'Yes I can. The feathers of its tail are very long.'

The broad, dark tail feathers hung down like an elaborately fashioned evening skirt. The bird's head was capped with black feathers, its neck had patches of yellow and red. The white breast appeared glossy in the bright tropical sunlight. When the bird flew to another tree the long tail feathers streamed out behind it.

Usai lowered his binoculars and breathed deeply. He smiled.

'You are happy to have seen this bird,' said Amai, misunderstanding.

'Yes I am very happy, Amai.' But it was not the whydah bird he was thinking of, it was Neli.

Close by, Mahachi and Chikomo were standing in the shallows. Each had a spear made from bamboo-like reeds that grew along the river bank. The two brothers walked slowly through the clear water, looking for pairs of bream performing their fatiguing dance.

'Over here Mahachi, a pair has just begun.'

They watched as the two fish worked in a circle, rapidly fanning the sandy river-bed with their tails, forming an indentation into which to deposit their fertilised eggs.

'It will be some time before they are exhausted and weak enough to spear. We must be patient,' said Mahachi. They stood watching, waiting. The sound of Lilmopane's laughter drifted over the water.

Mahachi looked towards the bank and waved to his grandmother. There was no response. He felt a light movement of air brush his face. It encircled him once, twice, enveloping him in a familiar scent, a comforting fragrance. The breeze wafted towards the long island and played among the fronds on the palm trees, before it moved away across the river. *Wood smoke and green soap*, thought Mahachi. He looked at his grandmother again. Ambuya's head had slumped to one side; her right arm hung limply, the tips of her fingers were touching the ground.

He stood staring at the scene uncertainly.

'No,' he whispered, as he walked slowly towards her in disbelief.

'No!' he shouted suddenly.

At the sound of Mahachi's voice the family turned towards him, watching in silence as he ran out of the water towards his grandmother. He knelt on the ground in front of her. Weeping softly, he lifted her limp hand and held it in his. 'Ambuya, Ambuya,' he said quietly, shaking her gently, 'do not leave us.' He looked at the beloved face. Her eyes were closed, her expression relaxed and at peace.

In the tree above, a Heughlin's robin sang sweetly; it was the totem of their people.